THE OTHER WOMAN
by NENIA CAMPBELL

Also by Nenia Campbell:

The Horrorscape series:

Fearscape

Horrorscape

Terrorscape

Escape

The IMA series:

Cloak and Dagger

Armed and Dangerous

Locked and Loaded

Cease and Desist

The Shadow Thane series:

Black Beast

Touched with Sight

Crowned by Fire

The Darkest Night

Star Crossed

Dragon Queen

Standalones:

Batter My Heart

Quid Pro Quo

Through a Glass, Darkly

Wishing Stars: Space Opera Fairytales

Poetry:

The Pocketbook of Sunshine and Rain

CAROL

TUESDAY APRIL 16, 1992

Up in the sky, the clouds were piled high and gray. Towering columns and minarets, wispy flags and banners: all gray, deeper gray, and every once in a while, a blinding white where the sun pierced through and scattered the brilliance of the light. It was the sort of reverential beauty that typically graced an album cover or a nature book, and Carol Clark was conscious of it, on such a deep and utterly profound level, that it felt nearly transcendent.

It was the sort of sky, she thought, that promised new beginnings.

As she drove, she looked at the dark teal of the water in the old gravel quarry as it reflected the rusting factory equipment and the splendid but slightly ominous clouds. She was sure the sky had been this beautiful before, but she rarely took the time to notice, just as she barely noticed where she drove or how anymore. How was it that some days, the world intruded, and other days, it did not? Sometimes she was only conscious of getting into the car and fumbling with her keys and then whole blocks of time simply disappeared. It was as if she had been in stasis, without any impression of time.

The hum of the car and the sound of the first raindrops pattering against the windshield were wonderful, comforting sounds. They wove in and out of the faded guitars of America's "Amber Cascades." The plastic of the cassette tape was starting to yellow from sitting out so much in the sun, but it was her favorite album of theirs, and she was happy to be awake to the sky and the water and the light and the rain and the music.

Her day had started out in an ordinary way, which wasn't to say it was a happy one. She had awakened to the bleating alarm on Gerald's side of the bed. He didn't turn it off—he never did—so she'd had to get out of bed to shut off the damn thing herself. After that, she hadn't felt like she'd be able to go back to sleep, even though it was an hour earlier than she normally got up.

Feeling rather malicious, she had let Gerald be, and he had apparently fallen back asleep—if he had even awakened in the first place. He came flying down the stars at 7am, just as she was finishing up the morning paper. "Why didn't you wake me at six?" he snapped, which made Carol think, *You have an alarm clock.* A bit disingenuously, Carol had replied that she hadn't heard it go off, and that she'd assumed he was planning on going in late, to which he had scoffed.

It seemed to her that her and Gerald's lives were filled with small skirmishes where the whole goal seemed to be putting the other person at a permanent disadvantage, just to watch them suffer. He constantly recast his priorities to illustrate, in arguments, how few of his real desires were fulfilled, and why this was always her fault. In return, she liked to thwart him, to do the exact opposite of what she knew he expected, and then retaliating to his complaints with remarks like, "Well, you never said that was what you wanted, how am I supposed to know what you want if you don't tell me, I can't read your *mind*, Gerald."

This, too, was part of the game they played. It was a sly and subtly vicious game, like the game of RISK they had played in college that had nearly ended their budding relationship before it had even begun. But it was their game, and she supposed they would continue to play it until death do them part. She certainly hadn't planned on becoming the nagging wife, and she was pretty sure Gerald hadn't intended to become a bastard husband, but in their ever-evolving roles in the game of life, they had both settled into these parts with the same ease as a comfortable old robe.

God, it made her tired to think about Gerald. She tried to push thoughts of him away, to concentrate instead on the shifting greens of the hills that rolled along the sides of the valley, mostly in the shadow of the clouds but every now and then lit up in a splendid swath of emerald green or the Day-Glo yellow of mustard flowers. But it was no use:

the glorious spring of well-being she had felt evaporated like so much nothing.

Bastard, she thought, gripping the steering wheel.

It might have been different if she'd had more time to love him, or if he had been around to love her. But neither of them seemed to have any time for kindness or love. It was just another thing they shelved for later and then never got around to, like back issues of *National Geographic*, or jars of homemade jam. Perhaps that was the way it was for everyone now, in this day and age.

Carol remembered her mother making dinners every night. Real dinners, from scratch, that she spent all day cooking. And then she, her brothers, her mother and her father, would all sit down to eat together after smelling the wonderful smells wafting from the kitchen all afternoon. Bread and biscuits, a prayer of grace, stews, roasts, potatoes in butter, conversation, scalloped potatoes, trifle and cake for dessert. Her mother had served up such dishes night after night, always with a smile. Carol, on the other hand, couldn't remember the last time she had actually cooked a dinner from scratch. She couldn't even recall for certain when she and Gerald had last eaten together. He got home so late that he usually ate in the car, picking up McDonald's or a sandwich while she had a frozen dinner and watched the evening news alone.

Her mother had lived in a completely different world. No one had expected her to work or asked her "And what do *you* do?" while expecting a long form answer. It was taken for granted that she was "just a housewife," just as every other woman on her mother's street had been a housewife. Carol, on the other hand, already had a job and ministering to her boss's needs left her no desire to further minister to Gerald the moment she walked through the door. Housekeepers could be hired for the home, but there were no *husbandkeepers*—nor, she reflected, would anyone want to hire one if they existed. That was the problem with young nannies. Giving another woman the key to your house was like leaving your car unlocked in a bad neighborhood: it was asking for trouble.

She pulled up to the curb in front of the house. It was a nice executive home with stucco exterior. They had bought it before it was built and she had watched it go up, astonished by the speed of its construction. She had been able to choose all the interior touches at the design center. Gerald had been in Hong Kong at the time working out some manufacturing problems for his company so she had been able to choose everything herself. (And what had he brought her as a gift, but a Chinese dress four sizes too small, which she had naturally taken as a dig at her own weight.) Her friend Diana had laughed when she saw Carol's house because all of the furnishings were white, although there had been a touch of jealousy in it. Diana had four kids and couldn't imagine trying to keep something so big pristine.

There were white carpets and tile, oyster walls, brocade curtains, and all the furniture, too, except for a wine-colored damask sofa, was upholstered in soft white cushions. It was immaculate only because she had a cleaner in once a week. It probably would have been immaculate anyway since they were never home. She unlocked the door and stepped into the hall, punching in the alarm code and hanging her coat on the antique-style mirrored oak tree in the hall, that had verdigreed metal as its decorative accents. Then she kicked off her shoes by the door and put on cordovan leather slippers with a long, satisfied sigh.

A blinking light from the sideboard caught her eye. There was a message on the answering machine. She hit the "play" button and flinched a little when her own tinny voice flooded the hall; hearing her own voice on the tape always surprised her.

"Hello, Carol, are you there? It's me, Diana." There was a pause. "Oh, well, you aren't home. I don't have much to say. Just wanted to know if you'd like to go out for coffee sometime this week. Just leave a message if I'm not there." A shriek resounded on the tape. "Amy, no, no—*no*. Stop that! Mommy's on the phone—well, Carol, I have to go." The wailing in the background grew louder, insistent. "Talk to you later."

Carol smiled. Sometimes it felt good not to have children. Especially when she saw how tired Diana was in the evenings. And Randall, her husband, was no help at all. Diana did it all herself, which wasn't really fair. It made her think of that German word for feeling a twinge of pleasure in the suffering of one's friends. After all, she had wanted children so badly for a long time.

Gerald had always said they would have children. He had said it over and over for many years. It was always just "not the right time." Then a few years ago, he quit saying it. In fact, he quit mentioning children at all. It was just another thing that lay cold and hard between them, like a slab of concrete neither of them was capable of moving out of the way. Too much effort would have been required. Even touching each other, these days, felt like a chore. Accidentally, their hands would brush when she handed him his dry cleaning or passed him a part of the Sunday paper, but they had quit hugging or holding hands or even—really—looking at each other.

So, whenever a child screamed loudly in the grocery store and everyone glared at the parents, or whenever Diana was especially fed up and ranted away to Carol about her cantankerous brood, the small tight knot that Carol carried in the pit of her stomach eased a little. It was the same knot that ached when she saw women hand-in-hand with their toddlers in the park, or babies smiling in their mothers' arms, or small, clean-cut children shopping in the supermarkets with their heads bent towards their mothers when asked what kind of lunch meat they wanted in their sandwiches. Yes, the schadenfreude—that was the word, she just remembered—eased the knot, but it was never really gone.

Carol went upstairs to the master bedroom and hung her work suit behind the bathroom door. She put her blouse in the dry-cleaning bag and threw her underwear in the net bag she kept on the doorknob for her delicates. She turned on the faucet in the whirlpool bath and climbed up the steps to the bath, taking care with her knees as she bent to put in the bath salts. Then she got in and rested her neck on the bath pillow. She could feel the soft caress of the rising steam as the warmth of the water penetrated her skin.

It was a lovely bathroom, she thought. Her work, too. White with touches of green. Ferns on the deep ledge of the window above the huge tub. The accents were wicker: a hamper, which was really a large loveseat-like bench (with a seat that lifted and which Carol used as a hamper); a small wicker table by the bath that held a huge Chinese pot glazed in white, green, and pink, in which rolled green towels with white monograms and satin trim had been arranged into a bouquet. There were four framed Chinese prints on the walls in the same colors as the pot, which illustrated the four seasons.

Carol had found a beautiful square pottery bowl of lustrous white and green from the 50s that had cunning oriental legs and a Chinese character in the bottom of the bowl. And in this, she mixed green and white French milled soaps that were almost too pretty to use. She had found a matching vase, also with a Chinese character, by the same potterer—Roselane Pottery—which she had put at the edge of the vanity with silk ivy tumbling out of it in jaunty curls and spirals.

Her good mood from earlier was almost restored now that Gerald had faded from her mind. She decided to make a few phone calls. It was rather indulgent to have a phone in one's bathroom, but with both of them working, there were certain calls that could not be missed. She dried her right hand on the edge of the towel closest and reached for the phone book that she kept on the bottom shelf of the wicker stand, the edges of it slightly warped from water.

Humming a little to herself, she looked under "Painting—Contractors" and listened to the phone ring. And then there was a click and a man's voice said, "Hello?"

"Hello," she said. "Is this Ray Flock Construction?"

"Yes."

"Oh good. I'd like a free estimate for some exterior work."

"What kind of exterior work?"

He had a very nice voice, she thought. Very deep. Carol played with the water with her free hand, making small whirlpools with her fingers as she imagined what he looked like. "I want the entire house painted, I think. One base color and then two trim colors."

"Okay. We can set you up with an appointment. What times do you prefer?"

"I'd prefer evening or weekends."

"How about this Wednesday evening at six-thirty?"

"That would be fine," she said. "Our address is four-five-eight-seven Hummingbird Lane."

The man repeated her address, asking her to confirm it, before saying goodbye briskly.

Well, that would be fun. Carol made a little X with a pen over the ad for Ray Flock Construction and folded the phone book up with the pen still inside it. The book was filled with lots of other little X's, across a number of pages. She was always surprised about how many estimators she had seen. She would tell herself to stop, and for a while she would, but then the compulsion would hit her again and she'd find herself picking up the phone.

Her biggest fear was calling the same man out twice. That would be embarrassing.

Ray Flock was a nice sort of name, though. She hoped he was as nice as the last painting contractor she'd had over. His name had been Jim. Jim Knight, which sounded like the name of a good cop on a police procedural. He had stayed quite a while, even after he'd finished measuring and adding up figures on his calculator. He'd had a lemonade with her and told her all about his family. He had a mother in a nursing home recovering from a terrible accident. His father was a general contractor, and so were his brothers. They'd all been working in the family business for a while, but he wanted to strike out on his own. He'd seemed happy. She didn't think he'd just been being nice because of the prospect of a job (that time, for interior work), but he had been disappointed, even curt, when he left a message on her answering machine inquiring about whether or not she had decided to go ahead with the painting about a week after the visit. And Carol had been too sheepish to call him back up and tell him no.

There had been so many men. Most of them were clean-cut, athletic-looking men who were the complete opposite of her husband, physically. Wearing jeans or khakis, polos or t-shirts, and big thumping work boots or tennis shoes. They came earnestly into her foyer, usually intent on shaking hands and dealing out their business cards, never suspecting why they were really there. Even *she* didn't know why they were really there. She would never cheat—but sometimes she just got so lonely that the prospect of seeing a face other than her boss's or her husband's was all that got her through the day.

Carol let the water out of the tub and wrapped herself in her green cotton bathrobe. She twisted her blonde hair to squeeze the water out, glancing at herself passingly in the mirror. It surprised her, how old she looked. She didn't feel old—she felt the same inside now as she had in her twenties, before she had started to get dark smudges under her eyes, and the tiny lines bracketing her brows and mouth. She could still put on makeup to cover all that, but the creeping decay of her skin bothered her more every day. She had been attractive when she was younger and she knew it had made all the difference on any number of occasions. Now she could feel it all falling apart and that some day she would be like an old ruin of a monument that people spoke of, when they spoke of it at all, only to say things like, "You should have seen it when it was new."

Despite the warmth of her robe, she shivered.

Dinner was a Healthy Choice Yankee Pot Roast. She had a diet Pepsi with it and wondered, as she snapped open the can, whether

Gerald was going to be home tonight. She couldn't remember his schedule anymore. It was probably written down somewhere but she wasn't interested enough to look for it. She sat at the table, staring at the empty black plastic tray beaded with grease, and wondered what to do next. She could turn on the TV and watch some stupid comedy she wouldn't enjoy, or *Murphy Brown*, which she would, but sleep seemed like the best answer.

As she lay in bed, she looked out the large west-facing window in the master bedroom. It was 7:15pm, but since it was late spring the sun was only just beginning to set. The spring shower she had run into on the way home was clearing and the remaining clouds were turning into fantastic pinks, purples, and oranges that reminded her of spumoni ice cream. It was so lovely, her chest hurt. She felt like crying or calling someone up to tell them to look out at the sunset, just so she could share the experience with someone else, but there was no one to call.

There was never anyone to call.

When she was a young girl, she had loved *Anne of Green Gables*, and had fallen in love with the idea of a "bosom friend." But she had never had one. She tried to be friendly. She invited people home for wine, for coffee, for tea, but somehow, she never seemed to click with anyone. There would be invitations for a while, mostly on her end, and then it was like the friendships just ran out of steam. After a few pathetic phone calls and perhaps a few years of Christmas cards, the names would be excised from the phone book with the slight sting of failure and the feeling that she was worthless.

Diana was her closest friend and they had only been friends for a few years. Part of her wanted to call Diana out to look at the sunset, but right about now she would likely be middle of the exhausting process of putting all of her children to bed. She wouldn't appreciate the interruption.

Diana had a friend from elementary school she still saw from time to time. They weren't close but whenever Diana visited Southern

California, she stayed with her friend, or at the very least, had dinner with her. Diana had friends from college, too. Sorority sisters she kept up with regularly. They had even gone to a spa together a few years ago, leaving their husbands home alone so they could have a "girls' weekend." Carol, of course, hadn't been invited.

Maybe if she had been more of a joiner, she would have had one of those kinds of friendships. But all Carol did in college was study and work—and date, but that was work too, in a way. Working to weed out all the men who wanted nothing more than a quick one-night stand from the few who might actually be marriage material.

Carol had looked as seriously for a husband as she had studied, and Gerald had seemed so perfect when she first met him. Good-looking, tall, and serious, too. Because he didn't say much, she had thought he was deep. She'd imparted her thoughts to him, and since he had never said anything to contradict her, she had never considered that he might simply not be thinking at all, which she now believed had been the case. He'd been tuning her out instead of introspecting.

It was amazing, she thought, how people's own minds conspired against them. Nothing could be as self-destructive to someone as their own illusions.

And if she did start over, what then? What if she made the same exact mistakes? Since she hadn't realized what Gerald had been before she'd married him, what if she went through a costly divorce just to pick another Gerald—or someone even worse?

Rebecca, her secretary at work, had picked up a string of abusive boyfriends. Carol, sympathetic at first, had finally given up on solicitous advice and comforting words because she realized that nothing she said or did would ever make a difference. Her suggestions only irritated Rebecca and prompted the woman to tell her to mind her own business. It was like this was what she wanted. *How dare she make women so stupid*, Carol had found herself thinking, on more than one occasion. But now she wondered if she weren't equally as stupid, in a different and less obvious way. Maybe that was what had bothered her all along.

The phone rang twice, shattering her thoughts. She moved to pick it up but the ringing stopped and no one left a message. *Probably a phone solicitation*, she thought, annoyed at the interruption.

She rolled back over to her left side and looked out the window. The sun had set and the sky was almost dark. Only a hint of purple lapped at the horizon, fading to a deeper indigo where she could just make out the pointed arch of a pine tree and the silvery wink of Venus.

With a strange tightness in her chest, Carol turned away from the window.

WEDNESDAY APRIL 17, 1992

When Carol woke up to the alarm next morning, there was a message on the machine and no Gerald. She wondered how she had managed to sleep through the phone ringing.

She put the coffee on while she listened to the message.

"Hello." It was a woman's voice, one she didn't recognize, high and girlish. "You don't know me, but I'm a friend of Gerald's. Gerald is in the hospital at St. Mary's in Lutherville. It's right off the two-seventy. Take the Jackson exit and come about five stoplights. It'll be on your right—no, the left. The left. We're . . . I'll meet you there. Oh, and it's three in the morning right now and this is Tuesday night—no, Wednesday morning. Three in the morning. Wednesday. Uh—bye."

Carol frowned as she hit "save," not really sure why she was keeping the message when it sounded like such a scam. Call this number to prevent this hospital charge—only, the woman hadn't said anything about a charge, had she? And she'd mentioned Gerald by name.

A prank then? It hadn't sounded like one. No hushed giggling in the background for one, and the woman, while youthful, had seemed entirely too old for such things. Feeling a little worried now, Carol dialed information and got the number for Saint Mary's. Then she dialed the number she was given and waited for the hospital's front desk to pick up.

As she waited, she thought about The Journal. That was how she thought about it, in all caps. Just like a horror novel, because in a way, it had been. She had kept a journal back when she was still angry enough to care about the deteriorating state of her relationship with Gerald. In the journal, she would write about new and ingenious ways that Gerald might perish. Some involved her murdering Gerald in some insidiously clever manner inspired by the Sue Grafton novels that she'd been reading at the time, but most simply involved bizarre accidents. She remembered that she had imagined him squashed by a fallen window cleaners' rig, decapitated by a piece of glass that had fallen out of a high-rise window in one of the many cities he visited in the course of his work. Killed in an airline disaster—there were several possible scenarios for those, and Carol had found many more inspiring means of offing him simply by being attentive to the newspaper. In the end, each of these morbid vignettes had made her feel *something* for Gerald, even if it was just hatred. A few times, she had even imagined to shed a tear or two over these imagined tragedies, picturing herself as the grieving widow at his—obviously very tasteful—funeral.

Looking back on it now, she supposed that she had secretly hoped he might find that little blue spiral-bound notebook and confront her about it. She hadn't really tried to hide it. What purpose it would have served her to have Gerald read page after page of her twisted fantasies, she couldn't say, except that, in a sick way, it would have made her feel *seen*.

Eventually, after a few months of this journaling, she had discontinued the practice of killing Gerald off fictitiously and thrown the notebook away. Not because she was afraid of being caught by Gerald, but because she had simply stopped caring.

That was when she had started calling up contractors. Sometimes she still wondered what happened to it. Whether someone had pulled it out of the trash. Would they take it seriously if they did? Had she written anything identifiable? She couldn't remember.

Someone picked up the phone, saving Carol from herself. Barely waiting for that first hello to get out, Carol blurted, "Has a Gerald Clark been admitted to your hospital?"

She chewed her lip anxiously to the sound of rifling pages.

"No," the voice on the other end said. "We don't have a Gerald Clark in our records."

"Are you sure?"

"Yes, ma'am," the voice said, with a hint of impatience. "I'm sure."

Carol slammed down the phone.

There, she thought. *A prank is what it is.* What was this mystery caller trying to do, calling her up with a message like that? Trying to rile her up before work? Some people were honestly so sick.

But where could Gerald possibly be? She looked at the kitchen calendar, which had no notes on it. Gerald didn't really do notes. There were a few phone numbers jotted down on it, all in her hand, a couple of stickies, but nothing else.

She raced into Gerald's office, a place normally forbidden to her. There was a small calendar on the desk, a book lovers' calendar that was a Christmas gift from one of his work associates. Nothing was written on it, and none of the pages had been ripped off for a couple months.

The page was currently flipped to January 12th, which featured *The Awakening* by Kate Chopin.

Inside his hardwood desk, everything was neatly organized. Pencils and pens secured with a rubber band, a snack bag full of paperclips and push pins, and a small checkbook-sized datebook from Moleskine. Carol searched through this latter to get to April. Gerald had blocked out all his business trips with X's. He was supposed to be in Taiwan tonight, so why would he be here?

If he even is here.

She drew in a breath and tried to convince herself, once more, that it was a prank. That he was safely on a plane in business class, whiskey in hand, probably nagging the stewardess.

But it hadn't really sounded like a prank, no. It had sounded like trouble.

Carol took the stairs two at a time and threw on some jeans and a beige sweater. She set the burglar alarm and loped out to the car. Swearing a bit, she realized she had forgotten to bring her purse, so she had to go back into the house to get it, nearly forgetting to disable the burglar alarm on the way in. She was angry and confused, and she knew she would have to be careful driving. She was in the sort of mental state that she scorned in other people: out of control.

Before leaving, she called her work's voicemail and left a calm message stating that she was out due to a family emergency. For good measure, she paged her boss, to tell him the same thing.

As she crept through the rush hour traffic at a snail's pace, her mind was a messy jumble of thoughts. She was terribly curious about the woman who had called. Why hadn't she left a name? Maybe she was a prostitute? Without losing any of her anger or worry, she began to feel uneasy, as well. Gerald was exactly the type of man who would rationalize such a thing, she thought.

Sex with Gerald had never been very good for her. Not that there was much of it. Maybe that had been a problem for him. But having him grunting and sweating on top of her had never felt romantic. It wasn't that Gerald was physically unattractive, but there had been no joy for her in their sporadic couplings. She'd tried to moan and wiggle, trying for what she saw in the movies, but she was never very sure how convincing she was. Her mind tended to wander during sex and she suspected this was not a very arousing trait in a sex partner.

But Gerald had never said anything. He never bought her sexy lingerie or asked to try new positions. She figured it was best to ignore the whole thing unless he brought it up himself. If she brought it up and he was perfectly happy, then he would feel attacked. But that line of reasoning had been when they still touched. She couldn't remember the last time they had sex.

Oh dear.

Maybe had had seen a prostitute after all, just for the novelty of it.

Shaking her head, Carol drove around the hospital, looking for somewhere to park on the busy street. She finally found a place in what seemed like miles from the entrance. As she walked up the automatic doors, a man in a suit rushed past her.

At the front desk, Carol stopped to again ask about Gerald Clark. This time, after some prolonged finger tapping, she was directed to go to the fourth floor by a woman in brown lipstick, and Carol felt very frustrated. "So you *do* have a Gerald Clark," she said, exasperation seeping into her tone.

The woman looked at her strangely. "Yes, he's right here." She waved a hand at her computer screen with long pink nails, speaking as if she thought Carol might be a bit dim.

"Are you sure?"

"Yes, I'm *sure*," said the woman, who was now clearly irritated. *Definitely the same woman from before*, Carol thought. "I'm looking at his name right here on my screen."

"But he wasn't there before," Carol said. "When I called." She was beginning to feel like she was coming off as quite a nutcase. "Earlier this morning," she added helplessly.

"Well, there could be a lot of reasons for that." The woman was unapologetic. "He *is* here now."

Thanks a lot, she thought darkly.

Stepping off the elevator onto the fourth floor, Carol found herself walking out opposite a nurses' station. She went to the desk and waited as a nurse made some notes on a chart. The nurse, who had brown hair and wire-rimmed glasses, looked up at her and smiled.

"Can I help you?"

"I'd like to see Gerald Clark, please."

"Are you the sister?"

The *sister*?

Carol was stunned into silence.

Taking this for agreement, the nurse rose from her chair and motioned for Carol to follow, not waiting for a response. Since she was already some distance away and walking very quickly in her white Keds, Carol did not bother to tell her that she was not the sister and, in fact, that Gerald *had* no sister, thank you very much.

What in God's name was going on?

The nurse paused, standing by the door of a room, and held out her arm to direct Carol inside. There were several little areas in there, each with a curtain and a bed. Most beds had a human in them, hooked up to numerous hissing, beeping machines. "He's over here," said the nurse, before leading Carol over to the third bed from the door.

A young woman was standing by Gerald's bed. She stood patiently, holding his hand. Possessively, her eyes intent on his face. The smell of Opium perfume clung to her clothes, which seemed a bit too dressy for a hospital visit. When the nurse brought Carol over, the girl turned, putting Gerald's hand down gently. She came over and embraced Carol.

Carol stiffened. Who the hell was this person?

The girl did not seem to notice Carol's reaction. "I'm glad you came so quickly," she said. "They don't seem to know how long he'll last." The girl said this with great emotion in her voice, warbling like an old-timey starlet.

Carol could see her eyes were very red. She was lovely even in grief, but most people were lovely just by virtue of being young. Carol tried hard not to like her. She wanted to be angry.

"How exactly did you know . . . Gerald?" she asked cautiously. She had almost said *my husband* but for some reason, she had not.

"Well, Carol, he told me so much about you and I know he hasn't told you anything about me." *You can say that again*, thought Carol. "Gerald swore he would introduce us when he could, but he is away just *so much*. We were engaged and he was going to tell you at a big dinner he was planning for all of us at Chez Nous. He was going to invite my folks and yours and have us all together to announce the big news." Fresh tears welled up in her eyes.

"I'm sure he was," Carol said brusquely. Engaged? That bastard. So, who was *she*? Was this why they thought she was the "sister" at the nurses' station? What the hell was going on?

Carol could feel her face going numb and her eyes were burning but she didn't want to cry. The shock of everything was catching up to her now and she could feel it like a lump in her throat.

"Do you mind if I sit down?" she gasped out, after an uncomfortable pause. "This has all been . . . really too much of a shock. Please tell me how this happened. How did Gerald end up here?"

She tried to distract herself with lists of things to keep her voice steady. The cleaning that needed to go out when she got home. The bills she needed to pay. The shopping—

"*Well*," said the girl (what was her name? Carol wondered), "we were watching Rocky on the TV—did you know that's Gerald's favorite movie? He just loves Sylvester Stallone."

Carol shook her head "no" and found it hard to believe that Gerald, who never watched TV or movies when he was home, had ever had such a thing as a favorite movie. She added a facial to the to-do list she was building in her head. She'd heard so many marvelous things about ginseng—

"Well, we were watching Rocky, and Dillon—that's my little boy—he needed a new diaper, but there weren't any. So, Gerald said he'd run down to the store and get some. And on his way to the seven-eleven, someone hit him and just . . . drove off. Hit and run, that's what it's called. How could a person do such a thing?" More tears. She reminded Carol of a Betsy Wetsy doll.

"I don't know." Carol sighed and wondered why on Earth Gerald was going to a 7-11 for this woman's baby's diapers. Did he have a son, as well as a mistress? "But what *is* your name, dear?" she asked, in a way that she hoped sounded sisterly. "Since Gerald never mentioned you."

"Oh, it's Melinda," the girl said. "Melinda Gray."

Carol paused and took a good look at Gerald's unconscious form. She'd been glancing at him periodically during her dialogue with Melinda, unwilling to look at him. He was covered by a light starched sheet. A tube snaked into his mouth and his lungs were being pumped up and down by a machine that made a rhythmic clacking and sucking sound. There were bags of stuff being dripped into him and bags of stuff being dripped out. He looked asleep, but his head was bandaged and there was swathing over his right eye. His arms lay at his sides and looked perfectly normal, although his hands were slightly curled and every once in a while, they twitched.

She shuddered. "Melinda," she said. "Can he hear us?"

"Oh, I hope so," she said earnestly. "The doctor says he can't, though. The doctor thinks he's already gone. But I have hope. They could be wrong. They don't know everything, doctors."

"What's wrong with him?"

"Um, his brain is bleeding. They told me they did something to drain it, but it didn't work. He has internal injuries, too, but they've fixed them or something. He was in surgery a long time last night. They wanted to know if . . . if he was . . . an organ donor."

Melinda burst into sobs.

Carol swallowed hard. "*I* don't know if he's an organ donor," she said hoarsely.

Melinda blinked at her. "Why would you?"

Shit. Carol felt ill. She didn't like blood. She didn't like talking about blood. And she especially didn't like the thought of Gerald's head filling up with blood. When she'd been writing in that diary about exciting ways to kill Gerald, she had never got as far as considering what it might be like sitting by what remained of Gerald *after*. Her killings, like the funerals that followed them, had always been sterile. Bloodless.

She had no idea what her own husband had wished for his last rites.

"Have you had anything to eat or drink?" Carol asked abruptly.

Melinda shook her head as she wiped at her cheeks, rattling some little bangles that Carol wondered, with a sudden lurch, if they had been bought for her by Gerald. "I didn't want to leave him, but the nurses brought me some ice chips."

"Let's go get some coffee," Carol suggested. "I saw a sign for a cafeteria."

Melinda looked hesitant, but Carol was forceful, so in the end, they went down the corridors, blazed with colored stripes that led you to your destination. Baby blue lines took you to maternity. Yellow took you to pediatrics. Green led to the ICU. A purple line led to the cafeteria.

Carol took a tray from the stainless-steel counter and got the coffees, some sweet rolls, two apples, and some bags of chips. She sent Melinda off to find a place to sit, not that there was much of a crowd. As Carol slid the tray towards the cashier, she felt as if she had stepped into another reality, into a life that was completely disconnected from her own. It was as if she were reading about herself in a book.

She found Melinda scrunched into a booth with her head resting on her arms. She looked worn out, which she must have been if she had been waiting up all night.

With my husband, Carol thought darkly.

A purplish tinge was developing around Melinda's eyes but her face was so lovely even when haggard that Carol felt a tenderness for the girl that she did not want to feel. She railed against it, trying to hold onto her anger at Gerald for enmeshing her with this creature. And now she had to tell her what Gerald couldn't himself: the truth.

"Melinda, we really need to talk a bit. Here, drink your coffee. You're going to need it. Do you want a sweet roll?" She could feel herself rambling. "Okay. Now, I guess Gerald told you that I was his sister, is that right?"

Melinda nodded tiredly.

"I'm not his sister, Melinda. I'm his wife. We've been married for about twenty years."

"What? *You*?" she said, with an indignation Carol really didn't care for. "I don't believe you. Why are you saying this?" Rapidly, she had gone from tired to outraged. A red flush tinged her pale cheeks. Carol put out a hand to restrain her, although obviously Melinda was going nowhere.

"I'm not trying to hurt you but you were bound to find out eventually. From his family, if not from me. And now there will be insurance and death certificates to deal with, and it's all going to come out, anyway." Carol dug through her wallet a bit desperately—it was a black and tan Gloria Vanderbilt clutch she'd picked up at an outlet in Napa. "Here is our wedding picture."

She held it out to Melinda.

Melinda obviously didn't want to take it, but curiosity got the better of her—and then, tears did. "Oh God," she said, looking away as if it were something dirty. "Oh *God*."

"It's okay, Melinda. Let it all out." Carol reached over and took one of her slim hands while sneaking a sideways glance around the room. There was no one very close and although a few people were looking in their direction, Carol supposed they would just interpret Melinda's outburst as some tragic hospital drama and not, well, a tragic hospital drama. Like *General Hospital*, but worse. God. She'd never wanted to end up like one of those sad sacks on *Jerry Springer*.

"Men are such shits," Melinda croaked.

"Yes," sighed Carol. "I suppose they are. Gerald certainly was."

The past tense, and its quick leap to her tongue, made Carol stiffen.

"I never knew," Melinda was saying now, in a rush. "I never suspected. God, I am *so* stupid. I am always so stupid." Her face crumpled and tears began to run from her tightly closed eyes. Carol let her cry for what felt like a very long time.

Hoping to head off actual hysterics, she said, "Where is your son right now, Melinda?"

"I left Dillon with Ann. She's my neighbor. She watches him while I work." She sniffled.

"When does she expect you to pick him up?"

"Oh, don't worry about that. I told her it was an emergency and she said she'd keep him for as long as I needed. We could tell from the wreck that it was gonna be bad, and I told her I needed to be here. He should have walked. I told him it was stupid to take the car. Why did he take the car?" she wiped her eyes with a napkin. "Did you love him?" she asked abruptly.

What a question, thought Gerald. And one she didn't need to ask in return because Melinda was clearly completely in love with Gerald. Or thought she was, which basically amounted to the same thing. "I don't know," she answered as honestly as she could. "I really don't know.

"I thought I loved him when we got married," she continued. "I don't know when that changed. But it did change into something more indefinite. Maybe it changes for all people who get married. I mean, part of what you love about someone is what you imagine about them. And once they are living with you *all* the time, not much is left to the imagination. Then you begin to study the other person, watching for their faults, and suddenly being annoyed becomes easier than ever being in love. Or maybe that's just the pattern we fell into. Maybe not everybody falls out of love. Maybe true love really does exist, though I doubt it."

Melinda looked doubtful. Doubtful that she, Carol, had not loved the wonderful Gerald? Or doubtful of the proposition that love was mutable? *She is, after all, part of that Melrose Place generation,* she thought. *All those teens hopping in and out of beds, thinking they're in love.*

Feeling truly miserable now, Carol took another stab at the issue.

"When I met Gerald, we were in college. And he seemed to be everything I wanted. He was kind and thoughtful. I thought we wanted the same things. But we didn't see each other all that much. We went out to dinner, to the movies. Things like that. I assumed a lot.

"I'll give you an example. We went to art movies and when he didn't say much, I thought it was because he had been as moved as I had. I thought we were sharing this deep, rich experience. But I found out later, not because he told me, but because I overheard him talking to his friends, that he hated most of those movies and he hated that I had made him go. He felt like he'd been *forced* to go. And then I began to wonder how many other things that I thought we agreed upon, that I thought we'd both enjoyed, had only been figments of my own imagination. I began to doubt everything and I guess at that point it became easier to find evidence of our differences.

"Once you start looking for differences, it's easy to find them. The hard things to find are the common areas. Looking back on it, I guess a couple really has to work at enlarging the common areas, because no matter how in love you are at the start, no two people are identical, and unless you work to grow into people who still love each other, I think most people will tend to grow apart. And Gerald and I didn't work at our marriage . . . and then we grew apart."

"But what about Gerald? Didn't he love you?"

"How can I answer that, Melinda? Especially since he was having a relationship with you? I think he loved me when we got married. Or at least, he thought he did. But I don't know anything now. Nothing appears to be the way I thought it was. And it really isn't the way you thought it was, either, is it?"

That was a bit cruel of her. Melinda seemed to think so, too. Her face flushed and she looked away.

"I don't blame you," Carol said, after a pause. "I don't even care that much, to be honest. Gerald was the one who lied. We both need to remember that. It doesn't make him bad. It just makes him a bit of a coward. Shall we go back upstairs?" she suggested abruptly, grabbing the coffee cups and napkins. Now that she'd unloaded on the girl, she felt a lot better.

Melinda nodded. Melinda obviously did care very much about Gerald and his lies. *Well, she would*, thought Carol. *I would have cared, too, when I was still in love—or thought I was.*

Melinda was still very much a child. Not a very innocent child, but a child nonetheless. It was difficult to imagine her as a mother. As they wandered back to the ward, Carol assessed her. She was smaller than Carol by a good four inches, about 5'5", and very slender. Her wrists, with their little bangles, reminded Carol of bird bones. She wore a dress with faded blue and pink flower print. Carol wasn't sure if the dress was fashionably faded or if it had simply faded in fatigue after repeated washings. It was hard to tell these days, with all that acid-washed denim and old plaid being in style. Kids went out into the streets with unwashed hair and called it fashion.

Melinda's hair was her literal crowning glory. It was wavy and golden and glowed even in the harsh illumination of the fluorescent lights. Her hair was abundant and tumbled nearly to her waist in silky falls. There was a seductive exuberance about it that contrasted with Melinda's quiet demeanor that she imagined some men must have found quite alluring.

Men like Gerald, apparently.

When they arrived back at the nurses' station on the way to Gerald's bedside, the dark-haired nurse waylaid them. "Will you please have a seat downstairs in the lobby?" she said firmly.

Melinda immediately tensed up. "What's the matter? What is it?"

"There have been some complications. A doctor should discuss it with you. I'm sure one will be down as soon as possible. Now please, go wait in the waiting area. We also have a chapel downstairs, if you prefer."

Oh shit, thought Carol. When they pointed you to the chapel, you might as well start planning the funeral. She had been invited to "wait in the chapel" when her father died. But she hadn't seen the point. She'd waited with him instead. Her mother had been too drunk to stay at the hospital and friends had managed to bundle her home, leaving Carol alone to stand for a vigil for her father while he died. She had stood there silently, holding his hand, the hand that had held her own little hand for so many childhood walks. The hand that had held her arm and gently passed her off to Gerald at her wedding. Her father's hands had seemed so young that even though he was certainly dying, it had been incongruous with the vitality still left in his hands. It had almost given her foolish hope. But die he did, and it had been left to Carol to make the funeral arrangements while her mother sought solace in the bottom of a bottle.

At least her father had opted for cremation. That had been easy enough to arrange. Gerald, she knew, wanted to be cremated, too. At least she knew that much about him. She might not have known about his secret mistress or whether he was an organ donor, or what songs he wanted played at his funeral, but she knew that much.

Numbly, Carol guided Melinda out of the first-floor elevator with its tinkling Muzak to the waiting area, pointing her to a couple of pastel upholstered chairs in a quiet corner. "I'll be right back," she said, before stepping away.

She went over to the information desk and noticed that the staff had changed. The cold and rather brusque woman with the intimidating pink nails was gone, to her relief. She told the ladies in cheery yellow scrubs that they were the family of Gerald Clark and expecting a doctor to come down and give them a status report. Then she went back to Melinda.

"Why don't you try to take a nap?" she suggested.

Melinda nodded and rested her head on the back of her chair, folding her arms over her chest as she closed her eyes. Carol picked up and put down an old copy of *Newsweek* that was titled *Kids and Guns*, and featured someone, rather inappropriately for a hospital waiting room, she thought, strapped to a gurney. She put it down and stared at the geometric patterns on the carpet. She found it rather impossible to concentrate.

Melinda had fallen asleep. Her breathing was regular and she was snoring gently. Carol watched her sleep. She tried to imagine Melinda and Gerald together. Was Dillon their love child? She had been wondering about that. Gerald had truly been a shit. If only he'd had the courage to leave her, she could have tried to make something out of her life, with someone else. But no.

Now she was stuck here with the remains of his life, literally and figuratively. If he had survived that accident, Carol would have been very tempted to kill him.

She looked down. Melinda's purse lay on the carpet near her foot. A little ruched number from Guess. Carol toyed with the idea of glancing through her wallet, just to see if she really was who she said she was. She nudged the purse, small and brown and slightly worn, but nothing fell out. She nudged it again, and this time the purse fell over. Nothing.

Not willing to commit herself to picking it up and rooting through it, Carol closed her eyes with a sigh and tipped her head back. The chair was remarkably comfortable for a hospital waiting room. *I wonder*, she thought, *what will happen now?*

A light touch on her shoulder made her bolt upright.

It was an officer.

"Hello," he said. "I didn't mean to startle you. I'm Office Muller and this is Officer Camara. We'd like to ask you and your friend a few questions. We understand you're friends or relatives of Gerald Clark."

"I'm a relative," said Carol. "I'm his wife. This is . . . this is a friend." She reached over to shake Melinda. "Wake up, Melinda."

Melinda opened her eyes and seemed to have a rather odd reaction when she saw the two police offers. She shrank into her chair and her complexion paled. She turned her face away.

"Melinda," said Carol, "these officers want to ask us some questions about Gerald."

"Okay," said Melinda, still not looking up.

"Officer Camara, why don't you take—Melinda, was it?—and I'll have a chat with Carol."

Melinda followed Officer Camara limply from the room, looking a bit like she was heading off to her own funeral. "Will we talk here?" Carol asked, looking around the waiting room.

"Are you uncomfortable here?" Muller sat down next to her. Rather presumptuously, she thought.

"No, this is fine. I just wondered . . ." She eyed him warily.

He was big and stocky, with huge forearms that reminded her of *Popeye*. His hair was receding a bit, revealing a reddened scalp, and he was very freckled. Around one of his thick and stubby fingers was a gold wedding ring. It glinted as he tightened his fingers around his pen.

"This is fine," she said again, after an uncomfortable pause.

Officer Muller nodded. "What's your full name?"

"Carol Michele Clark."

He wrote that down. "And your husband's?"

"Gerald Henry Clark." She tried to keep the same clipped voice she'd used before, but it was harder to say Gerald's name now.

"Who's Gerald's employer?"

"Westhover Industries."

Carol found herself getting rather perversely annoyed by the way that Muller held his pen. He was a lefty and dragged his meaty fist over the page of his notebook as he wrote, leaving his page and his hand slightly smeared. She nearly offered him one of the napkins she'd pocketed from the hospital cafeteria, before thinking better of it.

"His job?"

"Director of Manufacturing."

"Okay. Now let's go to your relationship with Gerald Clark."

"He was my husband."

His tawny eyebrows shot up. "You're divorced?"

"No, I meant, he *is* my husband—I'm sorry, we're still married." *And now they think I killed him. Oh shit. Oh shit.* Carol could hardly concentrate on Officer Muller's voice now.

"When did you last see your husband, Carol?"

Oh shit.

"Carol?"

Carol realized she was having trouble remembering when she had last seen Gerald.

She was having trouble remembering anything at all.

"Would you like something to drink while we talked?" he asked neutrally.

"No, I'm fine. Really. I'm just a little tired. Um, what was the question?"

"When did you last see your husband, Carol?"

"Yesterday morning," she said, after a pause. "Before he left for work."

"What time was that? Try to remember exactly."

"I'm sure he was gone by seven-thirty because I left him after that and I left at seven forty-five. I remember that. I looked up at the clock in the hall as I left. He hadn't woken up on time because he slept through his alarm, so he was later than he would have been if he'd left on time. He was very upset about that," she added randomly. "But that was because of the alarm clock, not because of me." Carol realized she was babbling again and repeating herself.

You are acting like a guilty person. Stop talking.

"Did you talk to him at all after that?"

"No."

Again, the eyebrows. "Was that unusual?"

"No, I just assumed he was off on another one of his business trips. He was supposed to be in Taiwan. I mean, I didn't know that before I heard he was here. I checked, after."

He paused, pen poised in hand. "How did you check?"

"Well, when I got the call that he was here—"

"Just a minute." Muller looked interested now. "Who called you, to tell you Gerald was here?"

"Melinda did."

"And your relationship with Melinda?"

"We just met."

"Here?" Officer Muller, though inclined to impassivity, registered some surprised at this. Carol felt an odd feeling of satisfaction. His stoicism annoyed her as much as the pen thing.

"She thought I was his sister, so she called me when she found out he was here."

"You talked with her on the phone?"

"No, I got a message on my machine when I woke up. It said to meet her here, to see Gerald. That he'd been in an accident. She didn't say what kind or . . . or how bad."

"That must have been quite a shock, Carol." It was a statement, but it was a question, as well. And possibly, Carol thought, still panicking, an accusation.

"Yes, it was. I didn't believe her at first. I called the hospital and they told me they didn't have a Gerald Clark, so I thought it was a prank. But I came here anyway to check because it didn't sound like a prank. I don't know why they wouldn't tell me he was here the first time."

"He was brought in as a John Doe, Carol. According to the hospital, Melinda showed up later with his identification. When we found out he had been identified, we came here to find out what he was doing when the accident occurred. He'd left his wallet at Melinda's apartment, so with no ID, he was brought in as a John Doe. They should have corrected the records as soon as Melinda brought in the ID, but you know bureaucracies. Mistakes get made."

Muller shrugged his shoulders impassively.

Carol stared at him, stuck on the words "left his wallet at Melinda's apartment."

So he really was having an affair.

"Do you know what he was doing on Broadmoor Drive in Lutherville at one-thirty AM, Carol?"

"No, I don't. Didn't. Melinda told me, I guess. Does that count?"

"What did she tell you?"

"That he was going to the seven-eleven for diapers," she said dully.

"Before talking with Melinda, did you have any knowledge of Melinda or of your husband's presence in Lutherville?"

"No. I didn't actually know where he was. We don't really talk much. But I thought he was in Taiwan before I came to the hospital this morning. I mean, after I checked his datebook. I didn't really know where he was before that, but sometimes when he gets upset, he just shuts down. I remember wondering last night where he was, but I was so tired, I didn't check. I really didn't expect him to be here." Her voice cracked.

"And you've been married since . . . ?"

"Nineteen seventy-two. June sixteenth, nineteen seventy-two. That's also my birthday. I mean the day, not the year. Not that you would think that," Carol added, feeling rather foolish but not being able to stop. She must shut her mouth. *Just answer the questions, Carol.*

Officer Muller looked the tiniest bit amused. "And the year you were born?"

"Nineteen fifty-two," Carol added again, pointlessly, "I'm forty."

"Did your husband have any disputes with anyone? Can you think of anyone who might want to hurt your husband?"

Apart from me? she very wisely did not say. "Not that I know of. But then, I seem to have been sort of clueless when it comes to Gerald," she said, with more bitterness than she wished.

"So, no fights with anyone or problems at work?"

"Like I said, not that I know of."

"Who did he report to at work?"

"Um, let me think. It was Henry. Henry . . . Gelgood."

"And what about other family members?"

"Well, there aren't any out here. The family is pretty spread out. His parents and one brother live in Washington—state. Then another brother lives in Idaho. And his oldest brother lives in Texas. I don't know about any other family. I don't have any other family myself, really. My parents are both dead and my brothers wander around a bit. I can give you a list of our family members with all their addresses, if you want."

"That would be very helpful, Carol. Any children?"

"No." Carol looked away and studied the corner of the upholstered chair Officer Muller was sitting in. It was very nicely made, the chair. A sort of tuck and role seam. Nice tweedy stripes, peach and aqua. They went well with the sherbet-colored geometric carpet. Considering how many people must have sat in this chair, it looked remarkably good.

"Other women?"

Carol jerked. "You mean besides Melinda?"

"Melinda?" Ha, she had surprised the impassive Officer Muller. Score one for her.

"Yes. Melinda is his girlfriend or fiancée or something. That's what she told me. Apparently, my husband had proposed to her."

He still looked incredulous. "But you didn't know anything about her before meeting her here?"

"No."

"And you didn't suspect that he was seeing someone else?"

"No."

"Has he ever seen anyone else during your marriage?"

"Not that I know of. But again, I may not be the best person to ask about this. After all, I didn't know about Melinda until today. I've no idea what else I didn't know."

"So, Melinda and your husband were having an affair and they were going to marry, but you didn't know about any of this."

Officer Muller stated this without any hint of skepticism, and yet, Carol knew he did not believe her. Carol was angry, furious. Even though part of her completely understood that this was unbelievable, she was furious. It had happened. To her.

"Well, really only my husband knew he was having an affair," she said tightly. "Melinda didn't know he was married, so she didn't know she was having an affair, either."

"And you told her you were Gerald's wife?"

Ugh. "Yes, in the cafeteria."

"And how did *she* react?"

"Well, obviously, she was upset. Anyone would be."

"And you, Carol—were you upset?"

"Well, yes, of course. I mean, I'd just found out that not only is my husband of twenty years likely to die, but he'd been seeing another woman. Of course I was upset. But I guess I was less upset than Melinda," she said doubtfully.

"Why do you think that was?"

"I don't know. I guess because she had all these hopes going forward and all I had was our past. Which wasn't all that much," she concluded sadly.

"So, you weren't happy?"

"I don't know. I really didn't think about it much. But that's the difference. Melinda thought about him a lot."

"And what were you doing last night?" *Oh God. See? See? He thinks you killed him. I ran over my cheating husband outside the 7-11.* It had a certain country and western je ne sais quoi. What a song it would make. "I Ran Him Over Like He Ran Over My Heart."

"I got home about five and I had some dinner and went to bed early."

"Did anyone call you? Did you see anyone?"

"I had some messages waiting for me on the machine and I listened to them, but I didn't call anyone. I'm sure my neighbor across the street, Graham Sterling, saw me. He watches everything in our neighborhood. If he was at home, he saw me. He's a writer. I think he gets material watching us all. It's kind of creepy, really."

Officer Muller asked her for the spelling of Graham's name. But she couldn't remember his address because she made a point of never looking at his house.

All at once, she remembered Ray Flock Construction. She could feel her face turning red.

"I forgot. I *did* call someone. I called a painting company about doing some work on our house."

"Do you remember what time that was?"

"Not really. I think around six?"

"And the name of the company?"

"Ray Flock Construction."

"So let me see if this is correct . . ." He read her rambling account back at her and somehow, it sounded even more ridiculous and surreal coming from him. "Is that accurate?"

"Yes, it is," she said meekly.

"Please sign right here, then." Muller handed her the clipboard and pointed to the line he wanted her to sign. "We'll be releasing some news on Gerald to the press. We hope we'll get another witness to the accident to come forward."

"You have a witness?"

"Yes, a Mr. Gumej Singh. He runs the seven-eleven. He saw the accident. He saw some of the license plate, too, and he gave us a fairly good description of the car. Unfortunately, he didn't see the driver at all."

"Oh. Okay."

Officer Muller stood up. "We'll be in touch. Here's my card in case you have any questions. Call any time." He offered his hand and Carol reflexively put out her own.

"Thank you, Officer Muller."

Officer Muller nodded again and left her. Carol watched as he went over to speak to the women at the admitting desk. She sat down again and tried to read a magazine while she waited for Melinda. Somehow, the words kept getting away from her, swimming before her eyes like floaters. She'd think she was reading and then after a page, she realized she hadn't taken in a single word. The words seemed to slip right out of her brain before she could process them. Nothing was making sense anymore.

The sound of female voices made her lift her head. Melinda was coming back with Officer Camara. Officer Camara smiled at Carol and she found herself smiling back, out of reflex.

The other woman was slender and dark, with a cap of curly black hair that looked like it had been permed, and white teeth that flashed brightly against her brown skin. Carol couldn't help feeling like she'd gotten the wrong end of the deal. She would have preferred to have been interviewed by Officer Camara than the slightly threatening Officer Muller.

Melinda did not look well. The smell of her perfume was beginning to fade and when she sat down, Carol got a whiff of sweat.

"It was awful," she said in a hushed voice to Carol after Officers Camara and Muller had left the lobby. "She was so pushy and invasive, asking all kinds of questions."

"Well, try to rest." Carol leaned back and closed her eyes. "That's what I'm going to do."

"What did you say to him?" Melinda whispered.

"To whom?" Carol asked, confused.

"The *cop*," she hissed, rather urgently.

"Pretty much what I said to you," Carol whispered back. Then she wondered why they were whispering, and she continued in a normal voice, "I told them I was his wife and that I'd only just met you. I told them what you told me. I'm not sure they believe me, but there's nothing I can do about that. Apparently, they have a witness, so that's good. And they're asking the community for help—so if anyone else saw the accident or recognizes the description of the car, well, that would be good, too."

Melinda said nothing more. But she looked tense and scared and something else Carol couldn't quite put her finger on because it was so ridiculous. Melinda looked almost guilty.

Carol wondered if Melinda blamed herself for Gerald's death since he'd died while sneaking around. Not that it was really any of her business what Melinda felt. The Other Woman, she thought. Who knew what a mistress really felt about her man?

The next thing she knew, a doctor was leaning over her.

"The ladies at the desk said you were waiting for news on Gerald Clark?" He was speaking in a low, grave voice. Melinda remained asleep. After glancing uncertainly at her, the doctor continued, "I'm sorry. I have to tell you he didn't make it. Despite our best efforts . . . he didn't suffer. I'm very sorry."

Carol thought about that phrasing. "Despite our best efforts . . . he didn't suffer." Did that mean they had wanted him to? She almost giggled and just barely managed to tamp down the rising feeling of hysteria threatening to burst out of her throat like a shaken pop can. She thanked the doctor for bringing the news in a sober voice she was proud of, glancing at Melinda.

There would be an autopsy, the doctor told her, to determine cause of death. Then the coroner had to be involved in some mysterious way. She didn't ask for details, cringing inwardly again at the thought of organs and blood. Eventually, the doctor told her, the body would be released back to her.

I don't want it, she thought childishly, but all she said was, "Thanks."

The doctor nodded and walked away, looking relieved. Carol shook Melinda gently by the shoulder. "Hey," she said. "Wake up. It's time to go."

Her eyes seemed to pen in slow motion, like a Disney princess. *Are those even her real lashes?* "You mean, go up to see Gerald? Is he better?"

"No, I'm afraid he didn't make it. The doctor just came to tell us."

"Which doctor? Are you sure he was talking about Gerald?"

"Yes, Melinda. I'm sure. He mentioned Gerald by name."

"But I want to see him. I can't leave until I see him."

"I'm not sure if we can see him. You wait here, okay? And I'll go ask if we can see him before we leave." She went back to the desk, braced for judgment. She thought it was a macabre request, but the receptionists didn't look shocked. One of them called up to the nurses' station and then informed Carol that they were expected.

Carol trudged back and collected Melinda again. Back to the elevator with the sleepy music. A nurse was waiting for them there. She led them in the opposite direction of what had been Gerald's room. She and Melinda were led to a room outfitted with all sorts of machines. The lights were very bright. Only Gerald's head was visible on the table where he lay. A sheet had been pulled over his body. *A shroud*, thought Carol, for that's exactly what it was.

Melinda flew over to the body and bent to give Gerald a kiss. Then she threw herself at Carol and began to cry as if her heart would break. Maybe it was already broken. Her cries wracked her entire body until she began to gasp like a beached fish. A nurse appeared with a paper bag.

"She's hyperventilating. Have her breathe into this."

Carol stuck the bag over Melinda's face, refusing to acknowledge how satisfying that felt. "Breathe into this," she ordered.

Melinda began to calm down. She looked peaceful and relieved.

Well, that made one of them.

■□■□■□■

Carol drove Melinda home. She couldn't think of what else to do with the girl and it seemed wrong not to offer, but she was already regretting it as the minutes ticked by in silence. Carol was so exhausted, so drained, that she didn't want to listen to a tape or talk or do anything, really.

Home for Melinda turned out to be a rundown apartment complex in Lutherville called The Palms. There were no palm trees, singular or plural. There weren't any trees at all. What there was were some shabby olive-colored bushes and some scraggly yellow grass, beaten to dirt in patches, on what passed for a lawn. Some unsupervised Hispanic children were pulling a dog around in a very old rust-colored wagon that was so bent out of shape that its four wheels were never all on the ground at the same time. It looked like it had been run over by a car: a thought that made Carol cringe internally. The children were laughing, and the dog endured its fate in noble silence.

Carol reflected on the fact that at any given moment, someone, somewhere, was in the middle of a tragedy. Whole countries were in the middle of civil wars, famines, or epidemics, while the rest of the world went on laughing or working, or playing or sleeping, and paying no attention. Pulling their wagons and having fun while the rest of the world was falling to pieces around them, for all they knew. There was something very, very disturbing about that.

Feeling Melinda's eyes, she tried not to stare at the Torino missing all its wheels that had been propped up on wooden blocks. "Is this your place?"

"Yeah. Do you want to come up?" Melinda offered reluctantly.

"No, thank you." She regretted saying this immediately because she *was* curious about seeing where Melinda and Gerald had spent their time, in their so-called love nest, but she saw no way to change her mind without looking foolish. So she pulled out a piece of scrap paper from the glove box and wrote her name and number on it with a dying pen.

"Call me if you need anything," said Carol. "Really. Anything at all."

Melinda nodded, taking the scrap of paper. She already had their house number—Melinda had called her at home—but she wanted Melinda to know that she was welcome to call.

"I'll be arranging things for the cremation today or tomorrow. Or as soon as I can. Do you want to scatter his ashes with me? I don't know when I'll get the . . . body. They'll do an autopsy on him and I don't know how long that takes."

Melinda nodded again, looking eager to leave.

"Okay. Then either you call me or I'll call you. Okay?"

Melinda nodded a third time, this time pivoting her body towards the apartments. Carol started her car engine and gave a little wave out the window. Melinda waved back. She was still there when Carol looked back in the rearview mirror. A rapidly diminishing figure making its way, ant-like, to the apartments, arms folded, with her halo of golden hair.

Melinda, at that moment, reminded Carol of pictures she had seen of women in the Depression. Perhaps it was just the dress and the way it whipped around her legs, and the beauty of Melinda contrasted with the grim surroundings.

Carol locked her door nervously. She had been too embarrassed to do it earlier, in front of Melinda, but she did not like this part of town at all. There seemed to be gang writing on every flat surface and all the homes had bars on the windows. Some even had barred doors. The industrial buildings were hidden behind chain-link fences and concrete fortresses, topped with snaking coils of barbed wire. It was nothing like Agua Verde, where Carol lived.

Agua Verde was a suburb. The town itself was very old, as the Mission of Agua Verde was one of the old Missions of the Camino Real, or so their realtor had been only too happy to tell them when they bought the house. The original town was very small and consisted of the mission, a historic railway station (no longer in use as a railway station, but now a Thai restaurant), and a main street of Victorian buildings painted in candy colors that housed antique stores, restaurants, and art shops. All the real business of the town was conducted at Mervyn's, Target, and Wal-Mart, or the mall. And all these huge buildings had been built right off the freeway, both to increase ease of access, and to hide the uglier side of Big Corporate America from the picturesque downtown.

The rest of the town was laid out in a lazy sprawl of varied housing developments. The oldest were small bungalows from the 50s that clustered about Main Street on roads named Yale, Princeton, Oxford, and Cambridge. Then there were developments from the 60s: stucco single-family homes, some with two stories, on modest lots. Building continued enthusiastically through the 70s but slowed in the 80s, as water became a problem and worsened with drought. Despite the town's name, there was not much *agua* to be found, except at the golf course.

Once in a while, in the middle of some of the later housing developments, one would come across a clapboard house. Sometimes these squatted on large plots of land, surrounded by gnarled oaks, and sometimes they were hemmed in by the modern homes pressing in on them like a pack of wild dogs cornering their prey. These were old Victorian farm houses that had once dotted the valley. Sometimes, Carol tried to imagine how it must have looked when there was nothing but white farm houses, with orange and almond and olive trees fanning out between them like the patches on a quilt. She couldn't decide whether it would have been pastoral or lonely.

Carol and Gerald had moved from a small home that had been built in 1971 in the tertiary layer of Agua Verde to a lovely new 4500 square foot executive home that had been completed in 1989. The lot itself was not that large, considering the size of the home, but neither Gerald nor Carol had any interest in gardening. After they put in a pool and a spa, there was only enough room for plantings around the edges of the yard, which suited Carol and Gerald just fine.

The house was Mediterranean in style, or at least, what the builder had decided was Mediterranean. It had a slightly sloped red tile roof and very light brick-colored walls, with the smooth columns and trimming around the windows done in a tasteful sandy beige. There was iron grill work accenting the windows and railings. The large mahogany entry doors had leaded glass inserts and matching sidelights and there was a matching leaded glass transom window above the front door. A bank of windows, all matching squares, looked out from the living room, which was at the front of the house to the left of the entry door.

To the right, as one entered the house, was a room that had served as Gerald's office, through which she had rummaged desperately mere hours (had it only been hours?) before. And it, too, had large square windows that looked out at the circular drive and the front of the house.

In between the living room and the office was a wide entry hall tiled in white marble. A large curving staircase led up to the master bedroom, the three upstairs guest bedrooms, and the rec room, which had a pool table that had never (to Carol's knowledge) been used. Of course, now she could imagine Gerald humping women on the pool table. Maybe he'd even had Melinda up there when Carol had been on one of her conference trips.

If one walked straight from the door to the back of the house, one ran into the large sunny kitchen and the adjoining family room. Between the family room and the formal living room was a small hall containing a butler's kitchen with a tiny refrigerator and a storage area for wine. This had seemed like an incredible extravagance to Carol, which was why she had ordered it in their plan. It seemed wonderful to be able to order something so completely unnecessary and still be able to afford it. There were also three fireplaces: one in the formal living room, one in the family room, and one in the master bedroom. Carol and Gerald never used these, either, but as with the wine fridge, it was exciting to be able to afford such excess.

The carpet throughout the house was a creamy white-textured Berber in a diamond pattern. Because it was so white, and the decorating scheme was so spare, the house seemed immense. And while this had never bothered Carol before, because she had wanted it immense, because she enjoyed the status, now that Gerald was gone, she wondered what she was going to do now in this huge house, all alone.

She could certainly afford it. Gerald had been insured for $850,000 and his company paid a death benefit of two years' salary. And she still had her job. But she must make no hasty decisions, she told herself, surprised to find that there were tears in her eyes. She decided that she must be more upset than she had realized, because right now, she didn't feel much at all.

Except shock. She felt a lot of shock. Especially about Melinda.

It could have been worse, though. If Gerald were still alive, then she would have had to face losing Gerald to Melinda. She would have had to sell the house—her house. The house she had built from the ground up. Every choice had been hers. She felt very violently that the house was hers alone. She would have hated Gerald for taking it from her, or giving it to Melinda. She would have had to be graceful during the divorce, while balancing on a tightrope of wounded pride and jealousy. She would have had to answer Christmas cards from clueless people and distant relatives thinking that they were still together, and make the decision whether it was worth it to correct them. Death was better than divorce, as long as you weren't the one who died, she decided.

She shucked off her shoes, and tossed the keys in a ceramic bowl that she'd centered on a doily to accent the credenza in the foyer. It was lunch time, but she had no appetite. Instead, she decided to just go right to bed. She pulled the shades closed in her bedroom and stripped off the hospital clothes, crawling into the cool Egyptian cotton sheets in just her underwear.

It was odd to be in bed in the middle of the day on a weekday. Somewhere, she could hear the droning of an airplane. She wondered where it was going? Was it bound for some exotic foreign location? Or was it just a routine domestic flight? A beam of light fell on her eyelids from a gap in the shades, and rather than get up and adjust them, she rolled over on her side.

Carol remembered walking home from school as a child, by a certain fence, when the sun fell just right through the gaps and stabbed into the corners of her eyes so that it lit up the blood vessels in fiery flares. She had been in sixth grade, then. She could remember the fence, and the feeling of the sun on her face, and the bright shaft of the sunlight as it hit her eye in a tangled jigsaw of yellow, red, and orange. She remembered thinking that it had been so beautiful it had hurt, the same way that she and her schoolfriends would cluster around a record player, and listened to music than just made them feel, and feel, and *feel*.

When did I become so numb? she wondered tiredly.

Finally, after much tossing and turning, she fell asleep. But it was not a quiet, restful sleep. It was a sleep filled with many strange dreams involving Gerald. Some of the dreams seemed to be about her notebook, which she had with her again for some reason. But Gerald was trying to get it, and she knew she mustn't let him have it, or something terrible would happen.

And then she awoke with a start to find the room darkening and tears running down her face. The doorbell was chiming. God, what a mess.

Carol tied on her robe and went to the front door. She looked out the peephole. A tall, athletic man stood on the porch. His dark hair was cut short, shaved along the sides, and she couldn't see his face very well since he was turned away. But his profile was handsome.

"Who is it?" she asked suspiciously.

"It's Ray Flock, from Ray Flock Construction. Is this Mrs. Clark?"

Oh shit. She had forgotten all about Ray Flock. Damn, damn, damn. "Just a minute." She hurriedly cinched her robe tighter. Then she opened the door, forcing a smile that snagged on her dry lips. "Please come in."

He looked at her in some surprise. "Did I get the date wrong? I had a note that our appointment was for six-thirty, Wednesday."

"No," she said. "It's . . . it's all my fault. I'm afraid my husband was in a terrible accident—well, was killed, actually, just last night. Well, he died today. The accident was last night. I only just got home from the hospital and all I could think to do was go to bed. I'm so sorry—"

Carol started to cry.

Mr. Flock was at a loss. Such situations did not normally present themselves to tradesmen out on simple estimates for exterior painting work.

He must have been a kind-hearted man, though, because he gently guided Carol over to the wine-colored damask sofa and sat her down, telling her to stay there until he came back with a drink. Normally, the thought of a stranger wandering around her home, with all its expensive things, would have propelled her from her chair and caused her to hover, but she was beyond caring.

After a few minutes, Ray returned with two glasses of an amber liquid and a glass bottle tucked under one muscular arm. By this time, Carol had managed to quit crying and switched to apologizing, but Ray commanded her to be quiet and drink, so she did.

Carol was not a drinker, except for wine, but the scotch had been just the right thing. What a clever man Ray Flock was, she thought. She looked over at him discreetly from under her wet lashes as she sipped her second drink. He had an open, honest, friendly face, which was probably an asset in his profession. People didn't let people into their houses who didn't look open, honest, and friendly. Was that really how he was, or was the face merely a mask to hide the demons?

After the second drink, she and Ray had a third.

Suddenly, Carol thought of how she must look. Her hand flew to her hair, still tangled from sleep. And her eyes would be all red and puffy from crying. And her crying face would have none of the tragic youthful charm of Melinda's. Carol feared she merely looked old and haggard.

Surprisingly, Ray laughed. "You must be feeling better."

Carol felt her face heat. She wasn't sure whether it was from anger or humiliation or both. "What's that supposed to mean?" she demanded, with all the dignity she could muster while three scotches deep and wearing nothing but a robe.

Ray, sensing her discomfort said, "I'm sorry. I didn't mean anything bad by it. It's just—when you put your hand to your hair, I knew you were thinking like a woman again. No, wait—that isn't what I meant either. I meant you were back to yourself. Yes, that's what I meant."

Ray nodded to himself. Ray and Ray were in agreement.

Carol wavered on the threshold of anger. It was the anger of foolish pride, of outrage that her pride and her vanity had been so obvious. It was the anger at becoming what she had scorned in others for so many years: a fool. Then she began to laugh. She laughed for a good long time, and at first, Ray joined her, as most people do when someone else is laughing. But when she didn't stop, his laughter diminished and he began to look almost as worried as when she had been crying.

"Are you all right, Mrs. Clark?"

"Oh, no, Ray," she gasped, in between giggles. "I'm not hysterical anymore. At least, I don't think I am. Of course, I could be completely out of my mind and just not know it. That's what happens when someone is out of one's mind, isn't it? But really, it was just so funny all of a sudden—me in my robe, you with the scotch, this whole damn situation. How many estimators turn up and find themselves in this situation? Can't be many, can it?"

"Well," he said. "Since you're feeling better, I'll just be going. Maybe I can give you that estimate another time, if you still want it. But I'll be honest with you, Mrs. Clark. Your house doesn't appear to be in need of painting. Were you just tired of the colors?"

Carol drunkenly decided to blame it all on Gerald.

"Oh, I was happy with the colors. It was my husband who wanted the change. He didn't like what I'd picked out and he was angry I'd done it behind his back. Now that he's gone—" she just barely managed to stifle a giggle "—maybe I won't have it painted, after all."

She was very sorry he was leaving. He really was attractive, like Richard Gere in *Pretty Woman*. His dark, close-cropped hair was graying a bit at the temples in quite a fashionable way; his shoulders were big; and the open-necked polo he wore accentuated his muscular neck. How did one even get a muscular neck, she wondered. It wasn't like you could do a push-up. Or a neck-up. Carol had never noticed Gerald's neck but she was pretty sure it had been nothing like Ray's, just as Ray's arms were nearly twice the size Gerald's had been.

She didn't feel at all guilty for admiring Ray, considering what Gerald had apparently been up to before his untimely death. If she could have, she would have asked Ray to stay for dinner, but she knew she was not up to cooking, and no one but she, and possibly Melinda, could possibly understand a woman indulging in that kind of flirtation the day of a husband's death.

After seeing him out, Carol unsteadily locked the deadbolt, turned on the alarm, and carefully climbed the stairs. She'd drunk more than she had realized. The ceiling was moving at a slow tilt, bobbing up and down like a merry-go-round. She let herself fall face-down on the rumpled bed, grabbing her pillow as if it were a life preserver as she tried desperately not to be sick.

Once again, she was troubled by strange dreams.

This time, she was in her home, but it was not exactly *her* home. It was larger than she remembered, the walls were different colors, and there were strange new rooms that seemed to have no end and filled her with a wordless, bottomless fear. As she got further and further into the house, she became hopelessly lost, until she ended up in an attic. The attic was dark and full of cobwebs and packed with old boxes. On a dressmaker's dummy in the corner was an old yellowed wedding dress. When she tried it on and looked at herself in an old cheval mirror, she could see herself clearly, but instead of her own face, she saw Melinda's. She twirled around in the dress and then, suddenly, she was not alone. A man stood in the corner, watching her.

He came to her and took her in his arms and danced with her around the attic. He was tall, for she had her face pressed against his shoulder as they danced, and he was crushing her in his strong arms in a way that made her feel a little dizzy. She could feel his huge hand at the small of her back, but when she looked up to see his face, the dream changed.

Now she was in her grandmother's little bungalow from the 1920s. She was on the oriental carpet underneath the huge mahogany dining table that had occupied the entire dining room. Lace hung down all around her, but she could see the legs and feet of other people from beneath. Her grandmother, grandfather, mother, uncles, and aunts. Then her father came and crawled under the table with her. He gave her a kiss on the forehead and sat cross-legged, the way she was sitting. "It will be all right, duck," he told her. "I'm here."

"But you're dead, Daddy," she said.

"I know," he said. "But I miss you. I miss my little girl."

Carol began to cry as her father hugged her to him. And then Carol woke up crying, for the second time, with a heaviness in her chest that felt just like a heated rock.

Carol went to the bathroom to splash cold water on her face. To her surprise, it was 6am already. Relieved that she didn't have to go back to sleep, she slipped on a pair of shorts and a t-shirt to go get the morning paper. As she walked down to the drive, she saw Ray Flock's truck parked at the curb. It was a white truck with RAY FLOCK CONSTRUCTION written on it in blue and a phone number printed on the side, also in blue, with a graphic she couldn't quite make out.

Carol approached the truck warily and saw Ray sleeping on the bench seat of his truck. He had rolled up his jacket and tucked it under his head like a pillow. She tapped the glass and Ray woke up with a start before cranking the window down.

"Er, hello," he said. "I bet you're wondering what I'm doing here."

She had been wondering that, but she shook her head politely as if strange men decamped in front of her house all the time. "I was just checking to make sure you were okay. Is there something wrong with your car?"

He looked sheepish. "No. I didn't expect to be here so late. I had too much to drink last night with you and I didn't want to drive home. I meant to just take a nap. I didn't think I'd sleep 'til morning." He blinked out at the trees, rubbing his head a little. "I have the worst hangover."

"Why don't you come in and have breakfast with me, Ray? You can have a shower, too, if you like."

He hesitated.

"Do you like eggs and bacon?" Carol pressed. "Bagels and coffee?"

"Bagels and coffee would be great," he said slowly. "And orange juice if you have any. And I think I will take you up on that shower. Thanks a lot."

Carol nodded, looking up, and saw a small gap appear in the shades across the street. She knew that Graham Sterling was watching her from his bedroom, the creep. Well, this would give him something to puzzle about for a while, she thought with relish. Graham was a horrible gossip and he loved to spy on the neighborhood and frequently spied on Carol. She'd caught him doing it, lingering over his trash, peering out from the columns on his porch. But up until today, Carol knew she had never obliged him by doing anything interesting.

After checking to make sure Ray wasn't looking—he wasn't—Carol waved up at the small gap in the shades across the street, flashing a cheery smile that widened when the gap disappeared. *Maybe he'll think I'm having an affair*, she thought wildly. *Or an orgy. Maybe he'll put the scene in one of his filthy, dirty books.* She hoped he did. She hoped he'd dedicate it to her. It would be all the more satisfying, she thought, since she wouldn't read it anyway.

As Ray showered in the downstairs guest bathroom, Carol got the coffee ready and toasted some bagels. When Ray appeared, wet hair dripping, looking so appealing that it actually hurt a little, the table was set and everything was ready, including her explanation.

"I'm so sorry about last night," she said, as he sat down. "Really, I'm not usually like that." She poured herself some orange juice from the carton on the table. "Yesterday was like a nightmare. A long nightmare without end—I didn't even realize a day could feel so long. And it was like it wasn't even really happening to *me* until you showed up. Somehow, you made it all feel real. Not you, personally, but just the fact that I had made the appointment, and it was something that *I* had made happen, made the whole day feel less like a dream."

Ray was in the middle of a bite of bagel so she continued.

"My husband was killed in a car accident and as it turns out, he had a mistress scarcely out of her teens and maybe even a child I didn't know about. Of course, she didn't know about me, either. The other woman, I mean. Or at least, she didn't know I was his wife. She thought

I was his sister. That's what the bastard told him—he doesn't even *have* a sister! And she thought she was engaged to him. Can you imagine? I had to tell her at the hospital who I really was. I was nice about it. Or I tried to be. It wasn't her fault, after all." She didn't mention the police. She didn't want Ray thinking she was a murderess who'd poisoned his coffee to get her kicks. "Anyway," she said, setting down the orange juice carton belatedly, "that's why I cried."

"Good Lord," said Ray. "You could go on one of those TV talk shows with a story like that. Maury Povich does them. I see 'em advertised all the time in commercials."

Carol had been thinking the same thing in the hospital cafeteria, but somehow hearing someone else say that made her feel more like a freak. She folded her arms. "Why would anyone want to tell a story like this to a bunch of strangers?"

"Well, I'm a stranger."

"I hadn't thought about it that way," said Carol. She was a little hurt that he still thought of her as a stranger, even though she supposed that's exactly what they were. "What about you, Ray? Are you married? I hope you don't have the kind of story that could turn up on a daytime talk show."

"Well, maybe I do. My wife left a couple years ago. Luckily, the boys were almost grown but it was still a bad time for me. She cleaned me out of most of my money and it made it hard to do my job for a while since I was dealing with so much. I had to get a loan from the bank just to keep working. I got most of that cleared up now. The sad thing was, one of the boys wasn't even mine—well, he was, technically. It was my name on the birth certificate and I've been his daddy since he was born—but she was his only blood relative. And she would never tell him who his father was. He had some trouble over that, but now he's doing fine. My youngest works with me while he goes to the junior college, and the other two are at UC schools."

"Maybe everyone has a story fit for a TV," sighed Carol. "No wonder those shows are so popular. I guess I'll have to start watching them."

They finished their breakfast in silence. Then the phone rang. Ray started to his feet. "I'd better go," he said. "Thank you for the breakfast, Mrs. Clark."

"Please, from now on, call me Carol."

"All right, Carol. Thank you for breakfast."

Carol wondered why he didn't say "call me Ray." Did he not want her to call him Ray? Was that too familiar? Or was he not thinking of her at all? Was she just an awkward potential customer who happened to be a lot more trouble than other potential customers?

Did he even see her as a woman?

She saw Ray out to his truck and waved enthusiastically after him as he drove away. As soon as he turned the corner, she began to wonder if she had waved *too* enthusiastically. Would he now think that she was desperate? Perhaps crazed by the death of her husband? Carol made a face as she went back in to check the message machine, the hub around which her life and all of its disasters now, apparently, revolved.

"Hi, Carol, it's Melinda. You said I could call—are you there? I guess not. Anyway, I'm glad we met. I wanted to talk to you about where we're going to sprinkle Gerald's ashes. Also, I wanted to know if you'd mind if Dillon came along. He and Gerald were pretty close and Dillon is confused about the whole thing. I don't think he understands Gerald isn't coming back. Anyway, I thought maybe he'd get the whole thing a little better if he came along. He's a nice quiet boy. He doesn't cause much trouble. Give me a call when you can. I'll be at work tonight at five, but you can reach me at Richy's Steak House or you can call me tomorrow. Bye."

She rattled off her phone number quickly before hanging up.

Carol replayed the message to write down Melinda's phone number and then pressed "save." Why did she keep saving these messages? She didn't know, but she felt like she needed to do it. Like it was proof that what was happening to her was really real.

Closure, she thought. That was what this was. *Closure.*

She cleaned up the breakfast dishes and wandered about downstairs, picking things up and setting them down. *I could watch Maury*, she thought, glancing at the TV with a shudder.

When she heard the soft knock at the door, she was relieved.

Once again, she looked out through the peephole. Part of her hoped it was Ray, although that would have been incredibly strange. Maybe it was a delivery, or one of her nosy neighbors. *Bingo*, she thought, looking at Graham Sterling. He was holding a newspaper.

She grimaced. Should she pretend to be asleep? He raised his hand and tapped again, and she wondered if he could see the shadow of her through the peephole. *Shit.*

Carol opened the door a crack. "Hi," she said expectantly.

"Morning," said Graham. "I wanted to give you my condolences." He handed her the paper. *Her* paper. She stared at it, flummoxed.

"Condolences?"

"Gerald," Graham said patiently, as if talking to a very stupid child. "He's in the paper. The accident? That's also in the paper."

"Oh," said Carol. "Well . . . thanks. Was that all?"

Graham looked a little disappointed, like he thought he'd be invited in. *Tough shit.*

"If there's anything I can do—"

What is this? Did he think she was a horny widow now? Oh please, let it not be that. Just because she had let a man in her home *one time*, now, suddenly, she was easy?

"Just let me know." He looked into her eyes. "I mean it, Carol."

"Uh, yeah, Graham. Thanks. I'm pretty busy this morning. In fact, I should get going. But thanks for coming over. It really—it really means a lot."

"I mean it," he said again. "Let me know if I can do anything."

Oh my God. She stared at him with rising impatience. "I'll keep that in mind."

Graham turned and walked back across the street. Carol closed the door but continued to watch him out of the peephole. Great, if he knew, then everyone knew. She would be talked about. Hopefully news of Melinda wasn't in the article or all her neighbors would be milking that for years. Why would the police release that, though? They wouldn't. Would they?

She ripped open the paper. Ad circulars fell about her feet. The accident was on page one. Why? Surely there were more important things going on in the world than the hit-and-run accident that had killed Gerald Clark.

Carol scanned the article—really, it was only a small paragraph in the bottom right corner. The bulk of the story was on page fifteen. That was good. He wasn't *really* front-page news. Most people would probably miss it. It sounded very unsensational, or so she hoped.

■□■□■□■

HIT-AND-RUN SUSPECT SOUGHT

Lutherville, CA—Mr. Gerald Clark of Agua Verde was killed in a two-car hit-and-run accident early Wednesday morning on Broadmoor Drive near the intersection of Pine and Broadmoor, authorities said. An unidentified driver of a late model gold-color sedan was traveling at high speeds north on Broadmoor in the left late at 1:28am when the car went out of control, crossed into Mr. Clark's lane, and broadsided Mr. Clark's BMW, according to Mr. Gumej Singh, who manages the 7-11 on Broadmoor.

The car then sped off, while Mr. Clark's car struck a telephone pole, said Officer Robert Muller of the Lutherville Police Department. The force of the crash caused extensive damage to the BMW, Muller said. Gerald Clark was taken to St. Mary's Medical Center with extensive head injuries and was pronounced dead at 11:50AM later that same morning.

Authorities are seeking information on this accident. Anyone who might have witnessed the accident or who has any information relating to it should call the Lutherville Police Department.

■□■□■□■

God. And there it was. She could not concentrate on this. She could not take this in.

Breathing heavily, Carol gathered up the paper and its ads into her arms and took the whole mess into the kitchen, where she stuffed it into a recycling bag, unable to even look at it.

Looking out the French doors and into what little garden they had around the sides of the pool, she felt calmed. The signs of life—the birds, the wind coursing through the leaves—helped her forget about Gerald and Graham and Ray and Melinda. The plants were growing tall against the fence and they were all flowering brilliantly, except for the irises, which had flowered earlier that spring and were now mostly spent.

Carol had planted hardy shrubs like euryops daisies, which had profligate yellow blooms, and potato vines that climbed the fence and spread massive clouds of foliage and snowy white blossoms above the planters. There was Mexican sage, which had huge purple spikes of flowers that attracted fat black bees, which Carol wasn't thrilled about but she had decided to let them be. She had put in butterfly irises and birds of paradise and calla lilies, because she had wanted the pool to feel like a tropical getaway, and she had edged the front of the beds with smaller plants because she had once harbored a dream of cooking large family suppers with fresh herbs.

That dream died a pathetic death, she thought. At least the herbs were thriving. Well, except for the mint. She'd been told it was hard to kill mint once it got going, but apparently this mint had been too tasty for its own good because it had been eaten to death by grasshoppers.

She wished plants would just get perfect and stay that way, but it seemed that just when you had them the way you thought you wanted them, they would spoil the effect out of spite. They would wilt or turn brown or smell funny or, worst of all, die. And then you not only had to dig them up, but you had to go shopping for something else to replace the gaping hole they'd left in your life. Like the scroungy brown beds where the mint had once lived.

No longer satisfied, Carol turned back to the house and wondered what she should do next. She had made a long list of people to call, but after Graham, she no longer felt like talking to anyone. Her thin reservoirs of patience had become dried beds. She had already left a message at her office explaining her absence, thank God, but she hadn't yet called Gerald's or his family.

She had not paid much attention to Gerald's family when she had married him, thinking that she was marrying Gerald and not his family. Foolish of her, really, since she had thought them cold and far-flung and not particularly prone to empathy. She wished she had paid more attention now. The fruit truly did not fall far from the tree.

Carol decided to erase Gerald from the house. She got a box of large black plastic bags from the pantry and marched up to the master bedroom. She started with his suits, which he had been particular about. They were all designer, because he said that the foreign businessmen he dealt with cared very strongly about such things. He had insisted that they be hung in their protective plastic dry cleaning bags, by color. Carol took the Armani suits off their hangers and mashed them into balls before throwing them into the bags. She did the same with his dress shirts. The Countess Mara ties resisted being balled up, so she threw the whole tie hanger into the bags. The belts and the belt hanger were next. Into the third garbage bag, she dumped his underwear and sock drawer and some of his shoes. She hoped the homeless ended up wearing all these clothes. Gerald had hated the homeless. Gerald had wanted the homeless all locked up where they couldn't bother decent, hardworking men of society like himself, who *had* jobs. Gerald was exactly the type of man to tell a homeless man to "get a job." How wonderful it would be for the homeless to be wandering around accosting other Gerald-like individuals while wearing Gerald's fine suits and hand-stitched Italian shoes. It was only too bad Gerald wouldn't be around to see the spectacle for himself. It would have offended him on such a profound and deeply personal level.

Carol smiled at the thought.

She dragged the bags downstairs and made a neat row of them by the door. She took the box of bags into Gerald's office. She was about to dump the first drawer of his desk into a trash bag when she realized some of the documents inside might actually belong to Gerald's employer and that they might be wanting them back. Reluctantly, she closed the drawer.

She scoured the rest of the house, not finding too many more traces of Gerald. There was nothing in the kitchen, except for a "World's Greatest Husband" mug that he had bought himself. It shattered quite satisfactorily when she threw it into the garbage can. There was a jar of Gerald's biscotti, which he liked to have with his morning coffee, but since Carol liked them too, she decided not to throw them away. He hadn't liked to share—and now, she thought, he wouldn't have to.

Looking at the bags in the hall, she felt a compulsive tickle to go through them again and make sure she hadn't accidentally thrown anything of her own away, but she knew she hadn't. Gerald imposed a rigid segregation of his things from hers. It was the same feeling that made her recheck the door six times or think randomly that she had left the garage door unlocked even though she hadn't gone into the garage. She could resist the impulses usually, but it took herculean effort, and her reserves were tapped. The sooner she got the bags to the Goodwill, the better. Then she could worry about other things.

Carol suddenly felt very tired. She went through the kitchen and rummaged through the pantry, before settling on a package of chocolate-covered almonds. She took those and a soda up to bed. She piled up all the pillows, including the ones that had formerly belonged to Gerald, and curled up with the almonds. In between eating, she dozed. She thought about all the places she had wanted to go, places that had seemed impossible or impractical, or that Gerald would have hated. She'd had to pass on a trip to Portugal because Gerald had thought there would be too many thieves. But now she could go anywhere she wanted, Portugal or otherwise.

But would she?

She felt almost paralyzed by choice. She didn't want to get out of bed even to brush her teeth, let alone fly to Lisbon. When the phone rang, she didn't answer it. She put her head under her pillow so she wouldn't hear the answering machine pick up. There was no one on the other end of that line who could have tempted her from bed.

She never put the pillow over her head at night. Gerald had always done that and it had made him snore terribly. Sometimes at night she would yank the pillow off, unable to stand the horrible gagging, choking, and snorting noises he made any longer. But she found she actually liked having the pillow over her head. It blocked out everything.

Carol awoke, with a choking gasp sometime later, with heartburn and a rotten taste in her mouth. When she ran her tongue over her teeth, they felt scummy. She tossed the now overheated, drooled-on pillow aside in disgust.

After brushing her teeth, Carol went downstairs. The house was already darkening as the afternoon faded into early evening. She had spent the whole day in bed. The black trash bags sat reproachfully by the door. *You had one thing to do today*, they seemed to be saying.

She walked past them and into the kitchen, flipping on the fluorescent lights. She heated up a frozen dinner, which she took, along with a very large glass of wine, back upstairs to bed. She didn't even bother with the bedside table; she just put the plastic frozen dinner dish on the sheet. She wondered how long her food would hold out if she did nothing but lie in bed and go on occasional sorties to the kitchen. Eventually, she supposed, she'd have to leave the house.

She grabbed the remote from Gerald's nightstand and turned on the news, but it seemed unimportant and completely disconnected from her life. What did she care if a warehouse fire had destroyed thousands of square yards of carpet? Did it really matter? The three-year-old drowning in its grandmother's pool was said, but why did *she*, Carol Clark, need to know about it? She hadn't a three-year-old and was very unlikely to get one in the near future. The weather—well, that might have mattered if she was planning on going out, but she wasn't. She flicked through the channels aimlessly, looking for something meaningful, something relevant. Home Shopping was good. But after watching Brenda, the blond, chatty, full-lipped host display a gold amethyst ring, a gold herringbone necklace, and a gold anklet (tacky, thought Carol), she became bored with the Sutter's Mill Spectacular.

Carol turned off the TV, put her empty frozen dinner plate on the floor, and put the pillow back over her head. She woke up very late to the sounds of shouting. She padded downstairs in the dark and saw the flashing lights of a police car parked in the street in front of her next-door neighbors' house. She watched out the window as the police tried to drag Lisa Youngman, the daughter of her neighbors, away from the front door.

Lisa was strung out on drugs most of the time, according to her sister, Megan (who was not supposed to tell people about Lisa, but she couldn't keep her mouth shut). It wasn't the stuff either, like weed, she had further confided to Carol, but the hard stuff. Street drugs, heroin, and even a little bit of meth. Trafficked in from Lutherville, no doubt, or other unsavory places from even further north. The Youngmans had had to take out a restraining order against Lisa. She had broken into their house and stolen all sorts of things. For drug money, Carol supposed. She had threatened Mr. Youngman with a knife, for money.

And once, when Mr. and Mrs. Youngman had taken Megan out to look at college for a weekend, Lisa and some of her friends had hired a truck from some shady Russians and made off with much of the Youngmans' furniture and appliances. Carol felt very sorry for the Youngmans but she felt sorrier for herself. She hated living next door to people with such liability connected to them. She had put in the burglar alarm because she had worried about Lisa breaking into her own home. It wasn't anything to do with her that Lisa had turned out so badly and she didn't like the continuing drama that resulted from Lisa's repeated attempts to come home. The Youngmans had chosen to have children and they had raised her, however they had raised her, and she had turned out this way.

Maybe it was their fault and maybe it wasn't. Carol certainly had her thoughts.

She saw a thin blade of light through the blinds of Graham's window across the street. So he was watching, too. Of course he would undoubtedly use this, as he used everything, for his horrible books.

He had given Carol a copy of one when she had first moved in to the neighborhood, which she had thought was both pompously arrogant and desperately needy. She hadn't been able to finish it. Graham was a science fiction *novelist* (or so he said), and claimed there was a deep psychological subtext in his books. She had heard him saying exactly that at one of their neighborhood block parties. Carol wasn't sure which book he had been talking about, but the one he had given her had been gruesome and repulsive. After reading the first couple chapters, she had graduated from a mere dislike of Graham to a grand and passionate loathing.

The lights shifted on her ceiling. Carol returned her attention to the window. The police car left; they had taken Lisa with them. After a few minutes, the little sliver of light in Graham's downstairs window disappeared before going dark.

Carol went back to bed and fell into a deep and dreamless sleep.

The morning was beautiful, sunny, cloudless. The hills, a brilliant green that only seemed to last for a few weeks out of every year. Whoever named the place Agua Verde must have arrived in the late spring, because for most of the year, everything was dull and brown and choked with tumbleweeds. As Carol stood at the window, she could feel the warmth of the day rolling off the hills and filling the valley. It almost made her want to go out and leave the house.

Almost.

She lay back in bed and tried to read *The Kitchen God's Wife*. She couldn't. She looked out the window. Nothing but blue sky and the occasional bird. She could feel time positively dripping. The beat of her heart, the slow tick of her pulse, the throb she could feel in her knee where her legs were crossed beneath the sheet. All seemed to measure out an infinite expanse. But it was not infinite, she thought. Time had stopped for Gerald and one day, it would stop for her.

Carol thought about God. Or rather, she thought about what she had once thought God might be. When she was young, she had imagined God as a sort of genie you called upon when things went wrong. "Oh God, if you help me find the dollar bill Aunt Evie gave me, I'll be a good girl forever." "Oh God, if you don't let me fail my math test, I'll go to church every Sunday without complaining." And then at some point, Carol had just stopped going to church and things hadn't been any different. Sometimes things happened the way she wanted them to, and sometimes, usually, they didn't. It all seemed to be just a huge cosmic farce that things happened at all.

According to the Youngmans, there was a God. A very strict, very paternal type of God who saw everything and weighed and measured everything a person did. The Youngman God was the only God. He was all-loving (as long as you did everything He wanted) but totally unforgiving if you didn't believe in him. Mrs. Youngman had tried on several occasions to get this across to Carol, usually after a very forceful invitation to come to their church. According to Mrs. Youngman, God was testing everyone. He was, thought Carol, certainly very busy testing the Youngmans.

But believing in that kind of god was worse than having nothing, Carol thought. She did not want to live in a universe where God tested you constantly like a divine sadist, probing and prodding you to find out how much pain you could tolerate. And the awful people who believed in that kind of God really deserved to be supervised by a benevolent jolly God who welcomed everyone—Hindu, Christian, Jew, Muslim, atheist, agnostic. That would be worse for them than if there were simply nothing. Because if it all ended in nothing, they would never suffer the knowledge of the error of their beliefs, and all their intolerance would be for naught.

But Carol felt pretty sure that there was probably nothing. She did not feel this in an empty, awful way. The realization did not frighten her. It was not terrible to be finite, to be small and limited. It would be nice, she supposed, to live forever. She would be able to read many books and fill her head with so much knowledge. But would there be any impulse to do anything if the infinite lay before her, or would she just lay about in bed wasting time, like she was now?

The doorbell rang.

Carol twitched. It could be someone awful, like Graham or the Youngmans. But it might be someone else. She put on her robe reluctantly and began the trek downstairs. She could see a tall figure in the dimpled glass insert of the front door. She looked through the peephole. It was Ray Flock.

She realized she had not washed her hair. She ducked her head by her shoulder and took a sniff. Oh God, she smelled awful.

She opened the door a crack and wished for a breeze. "Hello, Ray."

"Hello, Carol. I thought I'd stop by and bring you a little treat for your breakfast." Ray held out a bag. "I really enjoyed our breakfast together. Thank you for that."

Carol took the bag.

"I enjoyed our breakfast, too. Maybe sometime you'd like to come by for dinner? Lasagna is my specialty. Do you like lasagna?"

"I love it. But I'll eat just about anything." Ray slipped his hands into his pockets and looked to his left at a skateboarder coming down the street. The grate of the board on concrete ripped through the quiet like a knife.

"Well, that's great. Let's do that, then."

"Absolutely," said Ray.

"Well, I better go and get ready. I've got an early appointment."

"Okay, then," said Ray. "I'll give you a call later."

"Okay. And thanks for the—" What was in the bag? "Thanks for stopping by, Ray." He didn't seem to have heard her; he was already walking away. As he got into his truck, he gave her a wave over the roof and then he was gone. Thank God he hadn't asked what sort of appointment. She would have died before admitting that it was with the shower.

Carol groaned as she looked at herself in the mirror. Her hair was stringy and matted. But perhaps he hadn't been able to see that much of her hair through the crack in the door. There were splotchy stains on her t-shirt from the beef burgundy she had eaten in bed. But maybe he hadn't been able to see them. She had a pimple on her cheek, probably from the chocolate, but luckily it was on the side of her face that had been turned away. Hopefully he hadn't been able to see that, either.

She took a towel and put it by the side of her face, the way she believed the front door had been positioned. No, that didn't look too bad. And the front of the house was shaded by the porch, so it wasn't even as bright as the bathroom. Relieved, she threw her dirty clothes into the hamper and stepped into the shower. Her head had been itching and it felt wonderful to feel the hot water running over her neck and face. She lathered her hair up with Herbal Essence shampoo while the water ran over her like a rain bath. She savored the floral fragrance; it was almost like being in some magic rainforest, she thought.

She let the water stream over her until she felt the dull stiffness ease under the warmth of the shower massage. She thought about Ray. She wished she could take a shower with Ray; it had been a very long time since she had done something so intimate with a man. Then she looked down at her stomach, which bulged out a bit, and wished she could have her twenty-year-old body back and take a shower with Ray in that body. She really had to start doing *something* with herself. How long had it been since she could see her pubic hair? She sucked in her stomach. Why hadn't she noticed this? She remembered a time, not so long ago, when her stomach lay flat and didn't protrude at all, and she could look down the length of her body and it had been sleek and toned and tan.

When she got out of the shower, she stood in profile and sucked in her stomach again. The top part of her abdominal muscles complied but the bottom just lolled there above her pubic bone. She made a sound of annoyance and looked away, and noticed some Gerald items she had forgotten in her earlier purge huddling together in one small corner of the sink. She hurled the *Kouros* cologne and the electric razor into the trashcan angrily, before grabbing the phone book off their dresser and throwing herself naked across the bed.

She looked up health clubs.

Luckily, there were plenty to choose from. She decided not to call the ones with pictures of sleek young women in thong exercise suits on the theory that there might actually be young women who looked like that at those clubs. If those women actually existed, Carol did not want to see them or, more importantly, have them see her. They would probably laugh her out of the building.

She found a discreet ad for a family fitness center not too far from her home. She thought that sounded good. She made an appointment to take a tour and get a one-week free trial membership.

Carol got dressed in her sweats, thought about it, then dressed again in something nicer. After all, it was a small town. She could run into Ray, or someone else she knew. She picked out some jewelry—a gold tennis bracelet and diamond stud earrings—and put on some light makeup that she'd purchased after a shade match at the Clinique makeup counter. All nudes. She wouldn't want to look *too* nice. Ray might think she thought too much about her looks.

She went to the store to replenish the freezer. She bought Lean Cuisine and no chocolate. She did buy wine—both red and white—and some more of the scotch that she and Ray had had together. Between the two of them, they had mostly finished the bottle. It had been Gerald's, so of course, it had been expensive. She tried to think of it as an investment. She thought she saw Ray in the produce section. Her heart felt like it was going three times as fast as normal. It wasn't Ray.

Driving home, she kept noticing every white truck.

By the time she got home, she felt very foolish. But then a knock sounded on the door as she was putting the groceries away, and her mind immediately spun dizzily towards Ray. She opened the door rather breathlessly and found two young Mormons on her doorstep. The last thing she wanted to discuss right now was religion, even with two handsome Mormon boys in white shirts and pressed pants. The old Carol would have invited them in. The old Carol would have offered them food and nodded enthusiastically as they spoke, half-hoping that Gerald would walk in and make a scene. The new Carol thought the old Carol had been an awful, pathetic drip.

She would not be that way again. She would *not*.

"Sorry, I'm not interested," New Carol said. "Have a nice evening, though."

She finished putting away the frozen food and the vegetables. Fresh vegetables, not out of a can or a plastic bag, but real. She would have a big healthy salad for dinner, she decided, with fat-free dressing. She felt thinner already. She chopped and sliced and tore away until she had a mountainous salad. It made her think of Ray. She ate her salad as the evening news droned on about local fires and assaults and a silly human-interest story about a woman who collected things that looked like owls. *Another pathetic drip*, she thought. She could have been Owl Woman.

The phone rang, but it wasn't Ray. It was the Marina Hotel and Resort offering a free and fabulous weekend for two in Las Vegas for her and Gerald and *all* they had to do was listen to a very brief presentation. Carol put on her best bereaved voice and soberly informed the operator that Gerald was deceased that very week and she was finding this intrusion to be incredibly traumatic and painful. Silence on the other end.

"Hello?" Carol said tearfully.

A click, then dial tone.

Ha, thought Carol.

She finished her salad and went to bed early. This time, she dreamed of Ray.

Saturday morning, Carol found herself feeling much better than she had been for the last couple days. She had a mission now. Today was day one of her new life.

She got out some leggings and a pretty long-sleeved oversize shirt. As she drove to the gym, the thought crossed her mind that Ray might belong to one. She wondered if it were possible that he chose the family fitness center, perhaps to work out with the boys he'd mentioned. But it was more likely that he belonged to one of the gyms that had the ads for the women in thongs.

A woman named Chantal gave her a tour of the fitness center. Chantal was blonde and very perky. Chantal bounced when she walked in her tight khaki shorts and white t-shirt, which was emblazoned with the logo of the family fitness center and surrounded by colorful squiggles. Her little ponytail swished back and forth as she directed Carol to the various attractions of the club, which included a steam room and a juice bar. Carol decided she did not like Chantal.

But she did like the gym. She decided to start with the treadmills. She chose one on the second floor where she was all alone and could look out the window above the tennis courts, which had a glorious view of the hills and the clouds. "Don't Go" by Yazoo was blasting out over the oddly tinny speakers. She decided to go for time rather than do a hill course. She chose 3MPH as her speed. The sky was bright blue with a few puffy white clouds scattered here and there, and the tinny music was oddly invigorating after spending the last couple days in bed.

She was facing the northern hills of the valley and they were drenched in sunshine. She could see the reflection of her white cross-trainers in the full-length window, which the bank of treadmills faced. The feet in the reflection seemed disembodied, almost as if they were not her feet at all, but some ghostly feet completely unrelated to her. *The Phantom of the Family Fitness Center.*

Carol did thirty minutes on the treadmill and then, since there was no one there to see her sweat, she decided to do thirty more. As she was about halfway through, an older man with short-cropped white hair and very tanned skin began his workout on a treadmill to her left. She looked over at him briefly and he smiled. She smiled. She hoped she wasn't going to be expected to make conversation. But he had already put down a book on the shelf above the handrail and was looking intently at it. Carol, herself, was clearly forgotten.

Would he have made conversation if she was more attractive? She didn't want to be bothered and wasn't here to be picked up, but now she wondered if things would have been different if it were Chantal on the treadmill. Or Melinda. Would he have chosen the treadmill next to her then? Would he have chatted? She pounded the red STOP button before the thirty minutes were up.

In the lobby of the club by the front desk, a flock of ladies in tennis skirts were huddling together over a notebook while Olivia Newton John sang about getting physical from one of the open studio rooms. Carol wished she could wear tennis skirts. Well, she wanted to have legs like the ladies in the tennis skirts and *then* she wanted to wear tennis skirts.

For now, leggings would have to do.

She decided to buy a fresh strawberry fruit drink at the juice bar before going home as a reward. It was tangy and sweet and exorbitantly priced, and so cold it made the back of her throat ache. She drank it at one of the spackled plastic tables, watching the tennis ladies select Evian waters and acai bowls.

On the drive home, with the Lightning Seeds playing on the radio, she wondered how she could see Ray again. She wished she knew more about him. Then she could casually bump into him somewhere.

There were kids playing baseball in the cul-de-sac across from her house. She hoped they didn't hit their ball into any of the cars or break any windows. She'd have to schedule a repair. Suddenly, she had an idea.

She could throw a baseball into the back window. Then she could call Ray and ask him for a recommendation of a good man to fix it. Or was that too obvious?

Too desperate?

When she went into her house, she took a shower and decided to put a pin in the baseball idea.

First, she needed to call the crematorium and find out what she needed to do to get Gerald's body from the hospital to the crematorium. She wasn't sure when they would actually be getting the body since the hospital had to perform an autopsy and the coroner had to do something before it could be released. And she needed to get a copy of the death certificate for the insurance company, and for the bank to change the title to the house. There were a million faceless entities that all seemed to be notified about Gerald, and Carol could feel their weight pressing down her shoulders as they forced to her confront the reality of her situation over and over and over.

She decided to call Gerald's family first. She felt, very guiltily, that she should have done this sooner. Like days ago, probably. But there was nothing that could be done about that now. She wrote out a brief spiel on the back of an old shopping list, hoping fervently that she got nothing but machines. First, Gerald's parents. Not even an answering machine picked up. Such a relief. They were probably off on a cruise. Gerald's parents were frequent cruisers. They had been all over the world on cruises but had seen very little of it, aside from what could be viewed from a balcony or a porthole. They seemed to prefer it that way. Carol had been forced to look over their photo albums more times than she could count, and had been amazed at how many photos they had of themselves sitting at tables full of smiling strangers, drinking cocktails, or even just sitting by the pool in flowered shirts and muumuus.

She received nothing but answering machines at Gerald's first two brothers' houses, either. Unfortunately, the third brother's wife was home and picked up on the first ring. Carol, for the life of her, could not remember the woman's name. To her, she was just Scott's wife. It was, she realized with a lick of horrified amusement, a bit like *The Handmaid's Tale*. Ofscott.

"Hi," she said. "It's Carol. Gerald's wife." *Ofgerald.*

"Oh, how nice to hear from you. How are you?"

"Um, fine, thanks."

"How's Gerald? Is everything okay?"

"No, not really. This call is about Gerald, actually. He's been in an accident."

"Oh *no*. is there anything we can do? Should I call Scott?"

"No, there's nothing you can do."

"Do you need us to come out?"

"No!" said Carol. "No, no—there's no need to come out. He's already . . . well, he's already passed. I'm afraid he died at the hospital."

"Oh God, that's awful."

"Yes, it's been awful. Yesterday," she lied. "I'm afraid I've been sedated or I would have called sooner. I was just so, so upset." So many lies. All white lies, though.

And they were pretty good lies too. Women were always getting sedated on soap operas whenever someone passed. It made her wonder if someone ought to have given *her* something.

"Is there anything we can do?" Scott's wife asked. "Anything at all?"

"No, there's nothing you can do for me. Please tell the rest of the family that. I've tried to call but I just couldn't get anyone and it's been so exhausting, it's all I can do to call."

"Mom and Dad are on a cruise in China, you know."

Mom and Dad, thought Carol. "Oh, they are? I hope they have a safe trip. Don't tell them until they come back. There's nothing they can do now and it will only ruin their vacation. They might as well enjoy their trip." Then she added, "I should go. I have so many more calls to make."

"Well, take care. Remember to call us if you need anything, no matter what."

"Thanks, I will."

"Take care, Carol."

Carol still couldn't remember her name. "You take care, too."

She thumbed through her address book after hanging up. Maryann, that was her name. Maryann would inform the rest of the family. Thank God she wouldn't have to do any more family calls. She decided to call everyone else in the phone book who needed to be notified. Most of them would be at work right now and answering machines were easy to talk to. It was people who were awful.

It took her an hour and fifty minutes to work her way through the book. A few people weren't home and didn't have answering machines and one or two appeared to have changed numbers.

She decided to order a pizza for lunch. She had earned it with a good workout and from dealing with her emotional trauma. She would order one with extra cheese.

Carol picked up the phone and heard a bleep and then talking. Strange.

"Hello?"

"Hi," came Melinda's voice.

"Oh," said Carol. "The phone didn't ring."

But then it occurred to her a minute later that the bleep she had heard must have been the first tone of the ring before she had cut it off. Shit, talk about timing. Why did it have to be Melinda? she thought. Although it served her right for not calling the woman sooner and ignoring the desperate message she had left on the machine.

"That's weird," said Melinda. She sounded fine now.

"I'd just picked up the phone to make a call," Carol felt the need to explain, lest the other woman think she had nothing better to do than sit by the phone all day waiting for people to call her. "What did you need?"

"I just thought I'd check with you about Gerald when I didn't hear back."

"Yes," said Carol. "I was going to call, but his body hasn't been released yet."

"Well, I just wanted to check. I really want to be there. I really need to . . ." To Carol's horror, Melinda suddenly sounded like she was about to cry again, almost as if a switch had been flipped. "I really need to be there," she finished, in a hollow whisper.

"Of course we'll do it together," Carol said quickly. "I meant that."

She tried to sound sincere, but either it hadn't worked or it had, but too well, because Melinda began to cry on the other end. *Shit.*

"Please don't cry, Melinda."

Melinda continued crying—long, harsh sobs. She sounded like she was choking or laughing.

"I know it's hard," Carol said. "I know, I know." *Believe me, I know.*

Still, Melinda continued making noises.

"Gerald would want you to be happy," Carol said a little desperately. She wished she hadn't said it, even as the words were coming out of her mouth. Who the hell knew what Gerald had really wanted. Had Gerald even known? If he had known, wouldn't he have left her and made some sort of life with Melinda? He certainly hadn't given a damn about her own happiness.

Melinda was saying something now, her voice a crackle of noise in Carol's left ear.

"I'm sorry." She shook her head to focus. "What did you say?"

"I said, could you watch Dillon for a while, Carol?"

"I suppose I could," Carol said slowly. "Didn't you say you normally have the neighbor do it?"

"She has a job, and I need several days to take care of things. You were the first person I thought of, since you offered to, you know, help me out if I needed anything."

Fuck. "I have a job, too," Carol felt the need to point out. "But I am taking bereavement leave. When did you want me to watch—Dillon, was it?"

Melinda sounded better now. Composed. "Thank you, Carol. Thank you so, so, *so* much. Yes, his name is Dillon and he's three years old. How about this coming week? Maybe just Wednesday through next weekend? I just need to take care of some things."

"There really isn't much to do here, you know." Carol was already regretting her weakness in allowing Melinda to foist Dillon on her. When she had made the offer, she'd imagined buying Melinda's groceries or maybe picking up her dry cleaning. Not a week of free baby-sitting. She regretted picking up the phone at all. Actually, now that she thought about it, she regretted nearly everything about her short association with this other woman.

"He won't care," said Melinda. Which, Carol thought, was a strange thing to say.

"Okay. I suppose I could take him to a park. Do I need to pick him up?" She hoped the answer was no. She did not want to go back to that neighborhood with the iron bars and the gang signs.

"No, I'll drop him off. Thank you *so* much. Really."

"Okay," Carol said glumly, hoping Melinda would reconsider and knowing she wouldn't.

"See you, then!" Melinda sounded positively chipper now. Shit, shit, shit.

What had she gotten herself into? She didn't know anything about children. Why had she said yes? She didn't have to say yes. Why was she always agreeing to do things she didn't want to do? Now she was going to be stuck with this three-year-old for the better part of a week.

What would she do? What would *they* do? Why did Melinda trust her? She could be a child abuser, a Satanist, a crazy person. She could be mad with the desire for revenge.

Carol went to lie down, exhausted by the mere possibility of Dillon.

When she woke up, she called Maria, her house cleaner, to see if she could get an emergency cleaning. After several days of slogging around, feeling sorry for herself, the house was a mess. Luckily, Maria agreed to come after Carol explained the circumstances and offered to pay extra for the trouble.

If Maria was shocked about Gerald's death or the state of the house, she hid it well when she walked in through the door, toting her vacuum and her cart of cleaning supplies. But she was hard to read. Carol had given up trying to engage her in conversation long ago. Maria seemed to prefer it that way, which Carol tried not to take personally. Maybe it came off as condescending.

She decided to make a list of things to do with Dillon. She went into Gerald's office (no, *her* office, now) and found some paper.

Fun Things, she wrote at the top on the left, with several exclamation points. *Restaurants(?)* she wrote in the top right.

Restaurants were easy—there was a McDonald's nearby and they had Playland, so they could also be considered a Fun Thing. There was also Taco Bell, Lyon's, Burger King, and Denny's. That was probably enough. How old was Dillon? He still wore diapers. Surely, he wasn't a newborn. No—Melinda had said Dillon was three, hadn't she?

Carol made another heading in the middle of the page. *Questions to Ask Melinda: 1) How old is Dillon? 2) Who is Dillon's doctor? 3) Phone number to reach Melinda 4) Food allergies?*

Carol couldn't think of any other fun things. She was sure she'd seen TV advertisements for places with ball pits and colored slides, but she had always tuned out the commercials and none of the names were springing to mind, although they were probably in the phone book. She took her list to the kitchen and stuck it under a refrigerator magnet that looked like a croissant. She could add to it later, when she actually had the energy to deal with this.

The kitchen looked wonderful. All the countertops and chrome were sparkling. Carol could hear Maria vacuuming upstairs now. Perhaps Maria would know fun things to do with kids. Maria had a large family, although she wasn't sure just how large. She knew there were at least three daughters because Maria had taken calls from them over the years while at work at the Clarks'. One was named Juanita, she was pretty sure.

Carol decided to inventory the fridge.

She had no milk. Children needed milk. Even she knew that. She had fresh fruits and vegetables, but how many teeth did Dillon have? Would she need to buy baby food? She couldn't very well give Dillon tea and coffee and feed him on Lean Cuisines. She added to her list—*5) What does Dillon eat?*—and hoped Melinda wouldn't think it was a stupid question.

Then she wondered why she cared what Melinda thought was stupid. Melinda was leaving her son in the hands of a virtual stranger.

"I'm finished, Mrs. Clark," Maria called from the front hall. Carol took some money out of the Bavarian lusterware salt jar that hung beside the phone in the kitchen and put it in an envelope. "Thanks for coming at such short notice," she said, walking out. "You saved my life."

Maria accepted the envelope. "You okay, Mrs. Clark?"

"Oh, fine. Really, I am. Yes, I'm fine."

Maria looked doubtful. "So who is the little boy who comes over?"

"He's just the son of a friend of mine. She has to go out of town."

"You might want to move some of your things." Maria waved a hand at the general area of the living room. "Too much breakable."

"That's a very good idea. Thank you, Maria. By the way, I want to take him out but he's pretty young. I think his mother said he was only three. But there must be places around here to take kids to play—do you know of any?"

"Park," said Maria.

"Yes." Carol sighed. "I'd thought of that. Thanks again, Maria."

"See you next week," Maria said, her hand on the doorknob. Her voice rose slightly at the end of the sentence, almost as if it were a question. As if she had not been coming every week since the house had been built. And even before that, she had cleaned their small house. She had moved up with them and Carol had given her a raise because of the extra square footage.

"See you next week," Carol confirmed, finishing their ritual. And then she locked the door.

Sunday was a blur. Carol spent most of the day in bed. It was as if all the progress she had made over the last day or so had been erased. She thought about going to the gym, but it was a passing fancy, like thoughts of Ray, or cravings for the chocolate she now wished she had bought. She slept until evening, woke up late, and took a Benadryl with a small glass of red wine in order to fall back asleep.

On Monday, she went into the office to try and tie up the matters she had been working on before her life fell apart. Her co-workers were friendly and sympathetic but distant. She could feel their stares and had the feeling that they were sometimes talking about her before she walked into a room. There was an awkwardness between all of them now that was as sticky as clingfilm and provided just as much of a barrier. She had the feeling she would not be missed if she never came back.

Tuesday was a day of procrastination. Carol made lists of things to do and then did not do them. She paced the house, feeling as restless as a caged lion. Her eyes kept snagging on the list pinned by the little croissant. Until now, part of her had harbored some small hope that Melinda might come to her senses and bail out at the last minute, but that hadn't happened.

And now, tomorrow, Melinda—and Dillon—would be coming.

WEDNESDAY APRIL 24, 1992

Carol woke up with a start at 5am feeling as though there were something urgent she had to do. Then she remembered her phone call with Melinda and Dillon's impending visit, and she swore under her breath, pulling the pillow back over her face. Was he Gerald's? Would he look like a tiny Gerald? What if he hated her?

What if *she* hated *him*?

She thought she might call Diana. Maybe they could get together and take the kids to McDonald's for Happy Meals. Diana, Carol thought wryly, would be very surprised at the situation she had gotten herself in.

She got up and went downstairs to have breakfast, thinking how nice it had been to have breakfast with Ray. It had felt so intimate, as if the two of them were lovers. Maybe Dillon would provide her with an excuse to call Ray for help. Or she might run into Ray while she was out with Dillon. That could be good. Women always looked so appealingly womanly when they were out with children (provided, of course, that they weren't screaming at them). And she would not be screaming at Dillon, she told herself. No matter how much he tested her patience.

Visions of herself and Dillon floated nebulously through her head. No, he wouldn't hate her. How could he?

Feeling reassured, she cleared away the breakfast dishes. A glance at the knife block reminded her of Maria's advice to move the breakable—and dangerous—objects in the living room and family room.

Carol pushed the knife block out of reach and made her way into the living room. She moved the Baccarat cat, snail, and starfish off the coffee table and put them up on the mantle where they would be safe from little hands. She also put away the few Lladros that were out and moved them in with her main collection that she kept in the built-in china hutch in the dining room. She loved handling the

Lladros; they were so smooth and cool and beautiful. She had far too many of them already but she couldn't stop buying them. Each new addition seemed utterly necessary. It had all started with the bride and groom she and Gerald had received as a wedding present. That had started her collection before she even knew it had started and it had since taken on a life of its own.

The coffee table book of *The Birds of America*, with its watercolors by Audubon, was so heavy that Carol was pretty sure it would be safe. So she left that—maybe she and the boy could look through the pictures. And she didn't see what harm a child could do to the Deco brass ibex that stood by the hearth. The brass heron, on the other hand, stood three feet tall on the opposite side of the fireplace and had a very sharp beak which stuck straight out, unlike the ibex's, which was welded to the base. She shuddered when she thought of little Dillon impaled on the beak of the heron like a kebab. She moved the heron out to the large empty garage.

There, she noticed an oil spot where Gerald's car should have been: a dark splotch on the pristine concrete that she didn't like looking at. Would the car be coming back? She couldn't remember what had been said about the car. She might have been supposed to have it towed here, or perhaps she was supposed to collect it. Maybe it was being held as evidence. She couldn't remember anymore, which meant she would probably have to contact the police station.

Carol decided to worry about that later. She went back into the house, to her office, where she locked the door. Then she worked her way through the rest of the house, room by room, trying to imagine what dangers lurked in them for a child. Melinda had said he was three, hadn't she? But she was having a hard time visualizing him. Sometimes he was no more than a baby crawling from room to room, cherry-cheeked and smiling. Other times, she saw the dark child Gerald had been in photographs: unsmiling, even then.

The sound of the doorbell stopped Carol's peripatetic wanderings around the house. Dillon and Melinda were early. For one ungodly moment, Carol felt horribly awkward and unsure of what to do with her hands, in a way that she hadn't felt since she was a teenager.

You're a grown woman and you're afraid of a mother and child? Open the goddamn door, Carol.

She opened the door.

At first, she was so surprised, she forgot to greet Melinda. She had not imagined *this* boy, whose short dark hair stood up in wild little tufts on his rather large head, set on a spindly neck that did not look strong enough to support it. *He looks like an ugly baby bird*, she thought. He was pale, like his mother, but unlike her, there was no grace or beauty about him. His movements were jerky and he stumbled coming over the doorstep. He was painfully thin, almost pinched-looking, and he had dark bruises on his bony legs. The sight of the bruises gave Carol pause.

"Hi," Melinda said brightly, before she could speak. She set down a brown paper grocery bag in the hall, next to the black trash bags. *GROCERY OUTLET* was written on the bag. There were more shopping bags wound around her wrists from Sephora, Victoria's Secret, and Wet Seal. "What a wonderful house," said Melinda, looking around. She had been holding Dillon's hand tightly as they entered, but now she let him go with a rustle of plastic and he quickly disappeared.

Carol felt herself straining to listen to him, but tried to appear to be listening to Melinda, as well, who seemed to have completely forgotten about Dillon the moment she let go of his hand. She cleared her throat. "Are those for Dillon, too?" She reached for one of the plastic bags. "Here, let me give you a hand with those."

Melinda yanked her wrist back sharply, almost violently, and for a moment, the look on her face was—well, Carol did not quite know how to describe it. But she knew at once that she did not like it. For a moment, she had a flash of some cornered animal, teeth bared, but then

Melinda was smiling again. "No, sorry. Thanks, though. And thanks again so much for doing this! I really appreciate this. You really have no idea. Well, I'll just let Dillon get settled in—"

She turned herself to the door, moving her feet in her little green jelly mules.

"Just a second, Melinda," said Carol. "Before you go, I've got a list of things to ask you."

Wariness flashed over her face. *Aha, there's no escaping yet*, thought Carol. She went to the kitchen and ripped her note from the fridge with enough force to send the magnet flying. She was not entirely convinced that Melinda would not try to slip out the door in her absence. Quickly, she grabbed a pad of paper and pen from one of the sideboards before returning to the living room.

"Here it is," she said, ushering Melinda from the hall to the living room. "Why don't you have a seat and we'll go over this really quickly."

"Is it going to take that long?" The bags bounced against her legs as her shoulders drooped. "I'm not really sure what there is to go over."

"Are you in a big hurry? This won't take long—but I have to get a medical permission note from you and find out who Dillon's doctors are, and his dentist, and I suppose I should get an emergency contact number. And I wanted to find out what he likes to eat. Stuff like that."

Melinda settled warily on the wine-colored sofa, her gaze flicking and darting about the room. "Well, we don't really have a doctor right now," she said, tapping her foot in the mule. "We had one, but we moved, and Dillon hasn't needed a doctor. I guess you could take him to anyone nearby—not that you'll need to." She gave Carol an accusing look that Carol decided to ignore.

"I don't have insurance with my job. I'm just part-time at the restaurant. I don't get benefits, so I don't have an insurance number to give you or anything." Melinda's hands fluttered a bit in her lap, as if miming her lack of benefits. A scrap of lace slipped out of one of the bags and she tucked it back in. "If he needs a doctor, I'll pay for it," she added quickly, flushing.

"Oh no, don't worry about that," said Carol, also quickly. (*What are you saying?* said part of Carol's brain.) "I just wanted to know if there was any specific doctor. That makes it easy that there isn't, So, how about you write me a slip for Dillon saying something like I have the right to take them to the doctor or the dentist if he should need it. I don't think it needs to say any more than that."

She handed Melinda the pad of lavender-scented paper and the ballpoint pen. Melinda gingerly took both and jotted out a short note, in large, puffy cursive.

I give permision for Carol Clark to take my son Dillon to the doctor or dentist.

She signed it Melinda Gray. The dots over the I's were little hearts and "permission" was spelled wrong. Carol took the paper back without comment, although both of these things made Melinda fall a little more in her esteem.

"Could I have a phone number where I can get ahold of you—just in case?"

"Well, I don't know exactly where I'll be. I'll be traveling. I'm trying to take care of some loose ends, like I told you. But I'll call when I'm somewhere with a phone. I'll be back Sunday night, maybe even earlier if I can get everything done, although that probably won't happen. This is seriously so great of you to take Dillon." She got up as if ready to leave, tightening her grip on her bags. "I didn't know how I would get this done if I had to drag him along."

Carol clutched her list. "How about food? What does Dillon like to eat?"

"Oh, he isn't fussy. He'll eat just about anything. Burgers and French fries are his favorites. But he'll eat pizza, tacos, hot dogs, just about anything. But you have to watch him in the kitchen—he'll take the food. He'll hide it and then he'll eat it later. Or it'll just rot. Dillon," she called, raising her voice so abruptly that Carol flinched. "Come say bye to Mommy! She's about to leave!"

Dillon did not appear.

"And how old is Dillon again?"

"Three and a half," said Melinda. "Just like I told you on the phone. *Dillon*," she said, yelling now, "I said *come*. That means *now*."

Dillon did not come.

"Well, fine. If that's the way he wants to be, just tell him I left," she said crossly, stalking to the front door. "You should be glad you never had any," she tossed off over her shoulder as she swung out the front door. And then she was gone.

With my pen, Carol realized bemusedly.

That was certainly a different side of Melinda. She hadn't imagined that she had that kind of temper under what seemed like such a sweetly placid exterior.

"Dillon?" Carol called timidly. She was starting to realize that this whole meeting had gone off the rails in a way that was completely at variance with her plans. It made her anxious. She had hoped to have some sort of formal handing off, in a way that accorded her total control. She wanted Dillon to understand who she was and what was happening. Now she had to find the boy and explain the whole thing herself, without the help of his mother.

Would he cry? God, she hoped he wouldn't cry.

"Dillon?" She went from room to room, looking for him. He was not downstairs.

She looked behind doors, under furniture, in closets. Faster and faster, as she became more alarmed that he wasn't turning up. She imagined talking to Melinda on Sunday. *I'm so sorry, Melinda. I've lost your child. I think he may have starved to death in the linen cupboard.*

"Oh God," she said, feeling as if she were about a heartbeat away from tears. "Dillon, where *are* you?"

She found him at last in her bathroom. He was crouched in the tub, unscrewing a bottle of toothpaste.

"Dillon, please come out of the tub." She didn't quite feel comfortable laying hands on someone else's child.

Dillon ignored her. He was completely engrossed in the toothpaste. He squeezed the paste, watching it bulge out. Gently, he lowered his head to lick at the tri-colored log of Aquafresh.

"Dillon," she said. "Look at me."

He ignored her. Was he deaf? Melinda hadn't mentioned any issues. But then, she wouldn't, would she? *Now where did that come from*, she wondered, staring at Dillon. Another thought chased the first: *Isn't toothpaste poisonous?*

That jolted her into action. She took the toothpaste away and lifted Dillon out of the tub. He began to cry and tried to get the toothpaste back. Carol tossed it into the trashcan with Gerald's cologne and razor. Dillon squirmed. She got a firmer grip on him with her right hand and pulled him over to the sink. Wetting a towel, she tried to wipe the toothpaste off his face and hands.

"Nononononono," Dillon cried. He began to rock his head back and forth. His eyes leapt about from spot to spot in the room, but never on here.

"Look at me, Dillon," she said again.

He would not. Or could not.

She didn't force him. Instead, she waited.

Eventually, Dillon seemed to calm down.

Carol took him by the hand to the spare bedroom, feeling bizarrely grateful when he didn't try to pull away. She had done it up in purple accents, figuring it would be calming, with a lilac rug and framed Georgia O' Keefe prints of irises and morning glories. "This will be your room, Dillon."

Dillon went over to the bed and immediately looked under it. He sneezed.

Then he discovered the nightstand. He began to pull out the drawer and push it back in. Over and over. Once he pulled the drawer out too far and yanked it out completely. This made him cry. Carol put the drawer back in without a word and as soon as he could resume his little game, he was happy.

Carol left Dillon playing with the drawer—it wasn't heavy enough to hurt him, she thought—and went to call Diana. She barely waited for her friend to pick up before saying, "Diana, it's me, Carol. You've got to help me."

"Carol," said Diana. "What's the matter? Are you all right?"

"I'm baby-sitting and I think there's something wrong with the little boy, the little boy I'm baby-sitting."

"You mean he's sick?" Diana asked, sounding concerned.

"No, not sick. He's just acting funny." *And he has bruises on his little legs.*

"Oh, Carol." Diana laughed. "How did you ever get suckered into baby-sitting? How old is the little boy? I bet he's just being a boy. Why do you think he's acting funny?"

"He's three and he isn't a bit like your kids, Diana. At least, I don't think he is."

Diana laughed again. "Let's get together at the park. That will get this little boy out of your house and I'll get to meet him."

Carol heard a crash and a scream. *Oh my God.*

"I've got to go—park sounds great. Call me with the time. I probably won't pick up, so just leave the time on the answering machine."

Carol hung up on her friend's laughter and raced up the stairs two at a time. She found Dillon sitting on the floor, rocking back and forth. The nightstand had toppled over and the Tiffany-inspired glass lamp with its motif of grapes and grapevines was now shattered like bits of confetti all over the lilac carpet, interspersed with pieces of broken bulb.

Dillon had his head tucked down to his chest with both hands gripping his face, so that both his face and the top of his head were hidden from view. "Dillon, are you hurt?"

Dillon continued to rock, but Carol didn't see any blood, which eased her relief somewhat.

Very gently, she tried to move Dillon's head. He flinched and fought her. She had to keep pulling his hands down. But eventually, after a lengthy battle of wills where she would pull one hand down only to have another take its place, all she could find was an oval shaped lump on the side of Dillon's head.

Heaving a sigh, she carried Dillon downstairs to the kitchen, hoping to get him interested in drawing so she could clean up the broken glass from the lamp and bulb. But now, Dillon would not let go. She had managed to place him in the chair, yes, but his arms were looped around her neck, forcing her to double over with him clinging to her like a little monkey.

Carol could feel her back cramping up. "Dillon, please let go."

He didn't let go.

"Dillon, please, honey. Let go. You're hurting me."

His grip tightened. A wave of pain rolled down her spine like liquid fire.

"Ow!" she yelped. "Dillon! Let go!"

Finally, she managed to get his hands separated and off her neck. His eyes flicked to her and then away.

"Dillon, are you mad at me? Mommy will be back soon, I promise." *Don't infantilize the boy, Carol.* She cleared her throat. "But we can have some fun while she's away, can't we?" She thought her voice sounded high and desperate—pleading, almost. But Dillon didn't seem to be listening anyway. He was focused on the spoon he was tapping on the table.

She decided to just let him tap, hoping it would distract him long enough for her to get the Dustbuster upstairs. As she was pressing on the carpet to feel for any remaining slivers, she was stuck with a long shard that had embedded itself in the carpet. When she pulled it out, there was a bright red smear on the rug. Carol stuck her finger in her mouth and tasted the ferric saltiness of her own blood. She soaked the carpet with water, diluting the small spot to the faintest of pinks. *Good enough*, she thought, before running back downstairs. She'd never run so much in her life!

Dillon, thankfully, was still at the table. Now, though, he was tapping the spoon on her antique Spatterware bowl.

"Shit," said Carol. *Double shit. I shouldn't have said that.*

"Shit," Dillon echoed tonelessly, not looking up from the bowl.

Carol moved the bowl to the top of the refrigerator.

Dillon howled. He put the spoon on his forehead and ground it into the skin and screamed.

Carol grabbed one of her stainless pots from the hanging rack over the stove and put it on the table in front of Dillon where the bowl had been. Dillon went back to tapping. The howling stopped. There was a red mark on his forehead but it seemed to be just a pressure mark and was already fading. She'd definitely have to explain the bruise on his head to his mother, though.

She left Dillon at the table and went out to the hall. Briefly, she leaned against the wall to rally herself before dumping out the bag Melinda had brought. A little yellow cup with a white lid that had turned gray tumbled out. It had the faint picture of a bear on the side—not Pooh, but some generic but legally distinct equivalent, Carol thought. She put it on the floor next to her knee and it wobbled back and forth on its rounded bottom. *Weebles wobble but they won't fall down* ran through Carol's mind, but she couldn't remember why she knew that. What was a Weeble?

There were some worn clothes. Two t-shirts—one with a faded picture of Mickey Mouse's head, the other with a fat bear sitting with a honey pot. It looked like the one on the cup, she thought. Briefly, it occurred to her that they might have been part of a set. She folded the clothes carefully, before picking up a sleeper. There were holes in the toes where the brittle plastic feeties had worn out and it was badly stained. It should have been fuzzy but all the fuzz had been washed away a long time ago and now it was little more than a thin and nubby rag. There was a small pair of sweatpants. Gray. They had a hole in the crotch and were also stained. In the bottom of the bag were Dillon's diapers. Carol counted twelve of them and wondered if it would be enough. There was a scrap of gold terrycloth as well—it looked to be the remains of an old tea towel. Carol folded this carefully up, too, and jumped when a shadow fell over her.

"Baba!" Dillon had followed her and was now holding out his arms, wiggling his fingers with some urgency. "Baba," he said again, desperately.

"What's a baba, Dillon?"

"*Baba*," screamed Dillon. He shoved past her with more strength than she would have given him credit for, him being such a small and skinny boy. He yanked the scrap of terrycloth away from her loose grip and clutched it to his chest before burying his face in the dirty fabric. "Babababa," he said to it.

"This is Baba?" Carol gently pulled at the edge of the cloth and wiggled it a bit.

Dillon turned his back on her, pulling Baba away, still crooning to the cloth.

Okay, then.

As she studied his little back with the bony shoulder blades poking through the thin and stained white cotton of his t-shirt (which also looked about a size too small and left a gap between his pants and shirt), Carol had an idea. She would take Dillon shopping. Melinda couldn't possibly object. Not if she said that she knew Gerald would have wanted her to help out his son. Melinda surely would have taken—or may have taken—financial assistance from Gerald, so this was really pretty much the same thing. And it would be good for the boy to have new clothes that weren't ripped or stained or falling apart.

Would it look condescending, though, buying him new clothes without his mother's approval? It was as if she was saying his own clothes weren't good enough. Obviously, they *weren't*—but she didn't want to insult the woman. On the other hand, if she was going to be the one taking him out for the next week, everyone would think it was *her* fault the boy was wearing little more than rags. What a sight that would make. Just the idea made her cringe: her, in her nice jewelry and clothes, accompanied by a little boy in a suit full of holes. They'd think she was Mommie Dearest.

"Let's go shopping, Dillon," she said, putting her hand on his shoulder and gently propelling him towards the front hall. Dillon clutched Baba and allowed himself to be maneuvered, so she added, hastily, "Baba can come, too." Like there was any question of that.

Carol had Dillon sit by the door while she put on his shoes. There did not seem to be any socks to go with them, which explained some of the blisters on his ankles. The little things on the ends of the laces had also come off his tiny sneakers, so Carol couldn't get the laces through the last two holes because they were so frayed. Just before leaving, Melinda took Dillon's ratty t-shirt off and gave him one of hers. Gerald had washed it on hot with his towels by mistake. It said MTV on it, and she couldn't imagine where she had gotten it. From a coworker, maybe. On Dillon, it hung down to mid-thigh, but at least it was clean and covered his ratty pants.

Dillon didn't seem to have a serious attachment to his clothes, so she put his old t-shirt and other clothes back in the bag. She decided she would dispose of them tonight while he was sleeping. There was too much wear in them even for Goodwill. She knew people dropped their trash off at the Goodwill but *she* didn't like to do that. She would be able to tell they were judging her the next time she came to drop off a load. If Melinda asked what happened to Dillon's old clothes, she'd just tell her that they fell apart in the wash.

On the way to Target, Dillon kept undoing his seatbelt. Carol turned down Cyndi Lauper and pulled over to buckle him back in. But then he did it again. And again. After the fourth time, Carol held Dillon's left hand and blocked his right so he couldn't get to the seatbelt clip. Dillon wiggled and squirmed but did not manage to get out of his seatbelt—and all it took was driving one-handed. She turned into the parking lot and released his hand, wondering, as he immediately began to squirm again, if it was legal to duct tape a child into their seat. Probably not.

"Come on, let's go, you wiggly little caterpillar."

She helped him out of the car and then took his hand, which he didn't seem to mind. She saw her reflection in the glass doors of the store as they walked up. She looked like a mother with a child. Self-conscious, she pushed back a lock of her hair. It was too bad Dillon was dressed the way he was, but it was still fun to be shopping with a child. To have people think that she was his mother. Kind of like being an actress. She put on what she hoped was a motherly face.

And the Academy Award goes to . . . Carol Clark!

She put Dillon in the cart. He kicked too much to get him properly into the part of the seat where the buckle was, so she had to put him in the basket. He put a small hand on either side of the basket and immediately began to shake it, throwing his body back and forth.

"Stop it, Dillon," whispered Carol in his ear, keeping her motherly smile glued firmly in place. Other people were beginning to turn and stare, trying to figure out what the noise was all about.

The rocking got harder. Dillon looked up, past her ear, and grinned out into space.

Carol was floored by his smile. Lit up by the squiggly neon tubes mounted on the walls, he looked almost normal. No, not normal—that wasn't the right word. But there was a light in his face that she hadn't seen before. Was it . . . happiness? Did that mean he hadn't been happy before?

She felt guilty at the thought, like she'd failed him. Maybe she should buy him an ICEE—but, no. He was wired enough as it was and putting sugar into him might make him a little terror. Plus, what if he spilled the drink? Or got it on his face and hands? She still remembered what had happened with the toothpaste. This would be the same, except sticky and blue.

In the little boys' section, Carol lifted Dillon out of the car, amazed at how light he was. He felt like a bird, brittle and hollow-boned.

She held up some shirts to his back. He was a size ¾. She bought seven t-shirts in the most boyish colors—navy, green, yellow-and-blue stripe—and two polo shirts, blue and orange. She bought them all a little large so he would be able to grow into them. Then she pulled Dillon over to the shorts and got him two pairs of denim, some khakis, and four pairs of cotton knit in colors that matched his shirts. Since the boys' sweats were on sale (two for $9.99 seemed like a good price), she bought him two sweatsuits in two different shades of blue. She liked the colors and thought they would bring out his lovely eyes.

When she turned around to take him to the underwear, he was gone.

Carol raced around in a circle, looking in every direction. *How did this happen again?* Nobody had ever told her how quickly small boys could disappear. Had he been snatched? Kidnapped at a Target? It sounded ridiculous but such things happened every day. She saw them whenever she turned on the evening news. How careless of her to lose someone else's child. She would be held up as a laughingstock of a villainess, a total failure of a human being.

Carol saw movement at the center of one of the circular racks of clothes just as she'd begun to mentally construct her own moral obituary. "Dillon?" her voice rose. She could feel the waves of panic sweeping over her like a violent sea. "Dillon get back here!"

He was backing away from her out the other side of the rack, like he was about to run away. *Not today, mister.* She reached in and grabbed him by the hem of his shirt, pulling him unceremoniously towards her. Dillon flinched, ducked his head, and covered his arms. He looked like he expected her to hit him and was cowering to ward off the worst of the blows.

Jesus, she didn't want people to see this. To think it was *her* who had made him do this. But who had? Had Melinda ever hit him? Had Gerald?

Once again, she thought of the bruises. This time, with anger.

"Dillon," she said, very gently. "I'm not going to hit you."

She pulled his arms down from his face and knelt to his level.

"It's okay," she said. "I was just worried. I couldn't see you. I have to be able to see you. Okay?"

She hugged him. He hugged her back. Her heart melted. She did not want to let go.

"Come on, Dillon," she said tenderly. "Let's get you some socks."

In the sock department, Dillon fell in love with some cartoon X-Men underwear. "Honey, you don't wear underwear yet."

Dillon hugged the underwear tighter. His lower lip stuck out.

A woman shopping nearby decided to put her oar in. "You know, I bought *my* little boy underwear before he was ready. We put them at the top of the tank of the toilet so he could see every time he went to the bathroom. We wanted him to be motivated. Oh, and you *have* to get some Tinkle Targets. They are just the cutest things. You get them from the Smart Ideas catalogue. They are these little things you put in the toilet, planes and things with target symbols on them, and little boys have to aim at them. My son *loved* them."

"Thanks," said Carol. *You mad toilet woman.* "I guess we'll get the underwear, then." Turning to Dillon, she said, "Did you hear that? I guess you'll be getting your underwear, after all."

She smiled at him and he smiled at his underwear.

After getting some socks, a pair of Velcro tennis shoes (no laces to wear out, thought Carol), some sandals, and a huge package of diapers (just in case), Carol thought it would be fun for both of them to go look at the toys section.

She let Dillon wander from aisle to aisle. He still held his package of X-Men underwear, which he refused to let go of. When he got to the Star Wars toys, though, he dropped the underwear on the tiled floor to pick up a lightsaber. Carol put the underwear in the cart and watched him swing it. "Do you like that, Dillon?"

Dillon waved the toy in its package round and round over his head, knocking some Beast Wars figures hanging from the nearby shelf. Carol hung the packages back up on their metal hooks.

I guess that's a yes.

What they really needed were some sand toys so Dillon would have something to play with when they met Diana at the park. She was already imposing enough and it would be tacky to expect her children to share. *Where do they keep those damn things? Are they even in season?*

Dillon kept his saber as they wandered down the main aisle. She finally found them at the end. She decided to buy a giant red bucket of them that had other toys inside it, sealed in by mesh. It had a shovel (yellow), a rake (orange), a plastic dump truck (green and yellow), and some molds (a blue crab and a pink sun), as well as a purple trowel. Dillon paid no attention to the sand toys. He was focused entirely on the lightsaber. Carol decided to buy some bubbles and a big soft plastic ball. Every kid needed a ball to kick around, she thought.

And then she thought of all her antiques and hastily amended, *outside.*

She decided they should probably go home so she would have enough time to get Dillon ready. Everything seemed to take three times as long as she thought it would where he was concerned, and she wanted to make sure he was freshly dressed in his new clothes before they met Diana.

"Is it somebody's birthday?" the checker asked Dillon, who was still holding his lightsaber.

"Whish," said Dillon, waving it at her menacingly.

The checker turned to Carol. "Are you getting that?"

"Sure," said Carol. "I don't really have the energy to try and get it away from him."

"I know what you mean. My little girl is the same way. Sometimes I just don't have it in me to wait out a tantrum, you know?"

"Do you ever have trouble with your little girl undoing her seatbelt?"

The checker frowned. "How does he get at the buckle from his car seat?"

"He doesn't have a car seat."

Her frown deepened. "He looks way too small to be riding without one."

"Really? Well, I'm just babysitting him. His mom didn't drop off a car seat with him. Can I buy one here?"

"Sure, just a sec. Ma'am?" said the checker, whose name was Crystal according to her badge. She spoke to the woman behind Carol. "You might want to go over to register six. This is going to take a minute."

The woman behind Carol looked none too pleased to be sent to register six and shot Carol a dirty look. She smiled apologetically.

Crystal walkied over to the Infants section and asked them to bring up a child's car seat. "If there's one on sale, they'll bring that one."

"Thank you so much. I had no idea."

Several minutes and dirty looks later, a large box was brought up to the register by a boy who looked fresh out of high school. He was wearing a red Abercrombie and Fitch Rescue shirt that strained over his biceps. Like Ray, the boy also had a muscular neck.

Crystal scanned in the car seat. "Forty-nine ninety-nine and it's on sale."

Carol handed Crystal her Mastercard.

"I'm sorry. This one's expired."

"Oh, no it hasn't. You're looking at the issue date. The second date is the expiration date. You see, they printed the card all wrong. They should have put the expiration date first. That would have been ergonomic."

Carol looked at her blankly. Oops. No one ever knew what ergonomic meant.

"Everyone does that," said Carol. "I'm sorry. I try to tell people before they swipe it, but what with the car seat and everything, I forgot."

Crystal silently swiped the card again and punched in the second date. This time, successfully. "Here's your receipt," she said. "Sign this one, please."

$164.85. That wasn't too bad. And the car seat was basically half of it.

"Let me ask my supervisor if I can come out and help you put the car seat in," said Crystal. "They can be a bit tricky if you've never put one in before." She turned off the register light and went to a man standing up by the front in khakis and a red button-down shirt. A few minutes later, she came back. "He says it's fine."

They walked out to the parking lot. Crystal showed Carol how to install the car seat. Once installed, the harness was the only thing she had to buckle down. It was a large shield that came down over the chest and latched at the crotch.

"No way will he get out of that," Crystal said, with some satisfaction.

"Thanks so much. Really, I just really appreciate it. I'll write a letter to Target and thank them for your wonderful service. What's your last name?"

She folded up the box cutter and carefully put it into her pocket. "Rheberg. Crystal Rheberg. It was my pleasure. I'll just go ahead and take that box away from you." She gave Dillon a little wave, who was still occupied with his new saber, before turning and walking back to the store, lugging the empty car seat box behind her.

Dillon didn't even try to get out of the car seat on the way home. Either he sensed defeat by a superior enemy or he was too busy with his new toy. Carol wasn't sure which it was and it didn't really matter. The important thing was, she didn't have to fight and drive.

Perhaps it had been a mistake to agree to meet Diana at the park, though. Carol thought Dillon looked quite nice in his new clothes. She changed him in the parking lot and the difference between the old and the new seemed to make him a brighter, shinier version of himself. But he was still Dillon, after all, and when she greeted Diana and the kids with an almost desperate optimism, even she had to admit that the impromptu play date did not seem to be going well.

Diana's children were not out and out *rude* to Dillon. They were far too clever for that. Carol had never realized how devious children could be. Diana's children, the girls especially, simply made a point of being wherever Dillon was not. Looking from time to time out of the corners of their eyes at their mother, making sure she wasn't noticing or upset, and keeping a finger on the maternal pulse, they edged around the playground in their flowered dresses and pigtails, pointing and giggling meanly. They were always about fifteen feet from the boy, and every glance in his direction was usually followed by more whispers and laughter.

Carol might have found it fascinating if it didn't feel like such a personal affront.

Dillon seemed oblivious to the social machinations of Diana's girls and actually seemed to not notice the other children at all. Dillon was more interested in the sand. He tossed it up in the air in front of him, but since the wind was blowing towards him, it continually blew back in his face. The mere inconvenience of the sand in his eyes was not enough to persuade him to stop throwing sand. His new toys lay unused at Carol's feet. Although she had tried to get him to take the molds and try some of them out, he had no interest in anything but the sand.

Diana seemed not to notice Dillon or her girls. She chatted away about her husband and what seemed to Carol like exceptionally petty grievances: her nail stylist was talking about her in Vietnamese to the other nail stylists (or so she assumed, because she couldn't speak Vietnamese and why wouldn't they speak English if they didn't have something to hide?), the post office was charging too much for stamps, her neighbor was driving his car too loudly in the afternoons when she was trying to lay David down to sleep. Carol tried to listen but found it hard to concentrate on both the seemingly endless stream of words pouring out of Diana's mouth and Dillon's gradual progress on the playground. At some point, remembering herself and who she was talking to, Diana tried to commiserate about Gerald's death, but Carol had no interest in talking about Gerald *here*.

There was a pause in which she could hear the birds chirping from the bottlebrush shrubs lining the park. Diana was looking at her expectantly and Carol realized she had been asked a question but had no idea what it was or even what they had been talking about. The last sentence she had successfully taken in had had something to do with the traffic in the newly expanded downtown.

"I'm sorry, I just drifted off there. What was it you said?"

"I asked you how long you've known Dillon's mother."

"Oh. Not very long. She was a friend of Gerald's. He knew her better than I did."

"Someone from work?"

"Yes," lied Carol, unwilling to tell her the truth. As much as she liked Diana, she was a loose-lipped gossip, and the idea of Carol as the scorned woman would be too much to resist.

"So how long do you have him for?"

"Until Sunday. His mom comes back Sunday night, maybe sooner." *I hope.*

"He's a strange little guy. But it must help to have someone else in that big old house, to not be alone. Does it help?"

"Oh yes," Carol said insincerely, as if she needed help. Which maybe she did. Actually, she hadn't really thought about Gerald much at all today, until Diana had brought him up.

What she mostly felt right now was irritation and hurt. She knew Dillon was a strange little guy, but did one really come right out and say that about other people's children? Not that Dillon was hers, but what if he was? What if he was a relative? If he'd been ugly, would Diana have said, "Well, *he's* an ugly little guy?" Carol didn't think so.

It altered her perception of Diana in an irrevocable way to hear her judging this small and defenseless little boy, even—especially—if what she said were true.

Carol looked back towards the sandbox. Little David, Diana's four-year-old, was carefully digging in the sand, bending his neat dark head over his work with intense concentration. He was methodically filling his neon yellow bucket with his dayglo orange shovel, and then when it was full, he would carefully dump it out so that it formed a perfectly shaped mound. He had done this repeatedly, forming a large, circular fortress comprised of these little turrets, no doubt envisioning himself the king of this makeshift castle. He had adorned the tops of the towers with bits of twigs and pine needles. Flags, Carol supposed, glancing down at the toys still abandoned at her feet.

Dillon, meanwhile, kept walking backwards, throwing sand up in the air. He was getting perilously close to David's sand development. David, with his head down and his energy focused on the task at hand, possibly with the same gravity that his father brought to company boardrooms, did not seem to comprehend the impeding danger until it was too late. Carol saw it, but her call to Dillon went unheeded or ignored, and by the time she had gotten to her feet—curse her knees, dammit—Dillon had already squashed two of David's mounds with his little feet.

For a moment there was a deathly silence broken only by the chirping of the birds. Then David let out a wail and swung his bright yellow bucket angrily into Dillon's shin. Now it was Dillon who cried out, mostly, it seemed, out of surprise. Surprise that there were other people into whose path he had wandered. Surprise that these people appeared to have popped out of the woodwork, even though she and Diana had made a point of introducing them before setting them loose.

Then David went in for a second swing, which missed, as Dillon turned away, distracted. He lost his balance and toppled over, crushing several more mounds, which caused an increase in the volume of his screams. Diana raced over to comfort David, now weeping over the destruction of his kingdom. Dillon, on the other hand, had happily gone back to throwing sand in the air, though now at a considerable distance from everyone else.

"Ha," he said, as he threw the sand up in the air. Unfortunately, he often left his mouth open and much of it seemed to be getting into his mouth as he periodically coughed or gagged, before bending over to reach for another handful of grit.

"I think David's a little tired," Diana confided to Carol in a low voice, one of David's hands firmly gripped in hers. David was glaring tearfully over at Dillon who, naturally, remained oblivious. So, too, was Diana, despite her son being a little brute. She reached down and ruffled his hair. "I think I'll take him home now and put him down for a nap. It must be time for Dillon to have a nap, too.

"Girls," called Diana, looking over to where they were crouched beneath a bent pine. "Come on. Robert—" that was her older son, who had found a boy closer to his own age to play with on the jungle gym "—say goodbye to your little friend. Shoe time, shoe time, let's get our shoes on." She brushed the sand off David absently as she spoke, while Amy, Lisa, and Robert reluctantly came over and quietly put on their shoes. "Say goodbye to Dillon, kids."

"Goodbye, Dillon," the older ones chirped brightly, to please their mother. They damned well didn't do it for Dillon—and Carol was slightly gratified when Dillon did not acknowledge them and continued his sand-tossing game as if he couldn't care less. It was almost enviable, really.

She went over and took him by the hand. He shook her off.

"Come on, Dillon. It's time to leave." Relishing her spite, she did not tell him to say goodbye.

"Ha," said Dillon. Sand went flying up in the air in front of her. She could feel it hitting her hands and hair and closed her eyes, wondering how dirty that sand was with so many little hands and God only knew what else in it.

"All right, that's enough." Taking the boy firmly by the arm, she pulled him away from the sandbox and brushed him off on the grass area surrounding it before buckling on his new sandals. "Let's go see Baba in the car, okay, Dillon?"

"Baba cah," said Dillon. Was it a question? A sentence? Carol was thrilled. It was the most he'd said since he'd been with her. She would have to ask Melinda about Dillon's speech. She was sure he should be saying more at his age, but maybe he was just shy. Although she wouldn't have described him as quiet the way Melinda had. When he was upset, the boy could really scream, and he had a peculiar way of being able to communicate his wants, regardless.

Maybe if you were desperate for babysitting, you learned to describe your child as "quiet." Anyone would be happy to babysit a quiet child. Would anyone have been happy to babysit Dillon as advertised? As awful as it was, Carol suspected not. Although she was warming to him.

"Yes, Dillon. Baba's in the car. Let's go see Baba."

She got him settled in the car seat with his yellow terrycloth. The lightsaber remained on the floor, discarded. Dillon fell asleep on the drive home. Carol watched him sleep, completely and totally peaceful at last. His head lolled to the side, his hair stuck up against the back of the car seat, framing his head in a brown-black fuzzy halo. His eyelids had a purplish tint and his mouth hung open very slightly. He clutched Baba even in sleep, as if afraid someone would snatch the little scrap away from him.

He looked vulnerable, thought Carol, and so very, very young. Which he was. Obviously. But somehow, when he was moving around and causing trouble, Carol forgot how young he was and simply worried about what he was going to do next; it was as if he ceased being a child and instead became a force of nature. She got honked at in the left turn lane on Grove because she was so busy darting little looks at him in the rearview mirror that she had failed to notice the green arrow. She barely caught the light herself and smiled, pleased, when the honking car got stuck at the red.

She woke Dillon when they got home with a light touch on the shoulder and gently extricated him from the car seat. He followed her up to the house, hand in hers, rubbing at his eyes with one tiny fist. She made the mistake of taking off his shoes in the house. They were filled with sand. How could sandals hold so much sand? She wondered. They were open, weren't they?

"I think we should give you a bath. Come on, let's go. Bring Baba." It wouldn't hurt Baba to have a little bath, either. The yellow cloth was more gray than yellow at this point.

Carol made a little pile of his playground clothes and left them in the hall, where she could wash them later, walking Dillon to the bathroom in just his diaper, which was stretched taut and obviously soaking wet. When she took it off, she was amazed at how heavy it was.

"Wet," she said to Dillon.

"Weh," said Dillon, reaching out to touch the diaper.

"No," said Carol, yanking the diaper away. "Icky."

Dillon made a face, apparently familiar with the word 'icky.'

She got Dillon into the tub without any fuss. He obviously liked baths, as well as what her mother would have called "his business," which was the first thing he grabbed when he got in the tub. Carol decided to ignore that and put some bath crystals in the water. The warm odor of violets rose up with the steam, heavy and stultifying. Carol noticed Dillon was turning a bit pink. She felt the water and decided it was too hot and quickly added some more cold. Dillon seemed not to notice, still absorbed in his business. But Carol was worried.

Could I scald him with hot water? She wondered, watching him anxiously. Every room in the house seemed to harbor special dangers that had previously escaped her notice. She had seen a TV show once on kids who were killed in the home. One little girl had been strangled by a Venetian blind cord. Who would have thought of that? It was horrible. All these harmless household objects were just lying in wait to murder your child.

Not my child, she amended hastily. *Melinda's child. A child. Any child.*

She sat on the thick plush bath rug and squeezed water from a washcloth down Dillon's back. "Isn't that nice, Dillon? We'll be all nice and clean after our bath, won't we? You and Baba?"

He had let go of himself and was now chasing her lavender soap around the water: a task which he obviously felt required both his hands and his utmost attention. While he was occupied, she wrung out Baba and hung it over the towel ring to dry. The cloth looked a little bit less like a vector for disease, now. She was surprised Melinda hadn't washed it.

Carol couldn't believe she still had two days and a whole weekend to go. She was already exhausted. Maybe she could take a nap with Dillon after lunch. He didn't look tired, but then, *he* had gotten a nap in the car. "Okay," she said, trying to rally herself. "Let's get you dried off and have some lunch, okay?"

He let her lift him out of the tub and put him in a new diaper and one of his new khaki pants and t-shirts, which gave her a false sense of optimism that lasted just until they got to the kitchen.

Dillon did not like yogurt. He spat the yogurt on the table. He seemed to think the vegetables were toys, and maneuvered them, also on the table, as if they were little cars. He did drink some water and he ate about half a piece of bread. He wouldn't starve in one day but grocery shopping with Dillon was clearly the next major step to take since, contrary to what Melinda had said, he apparently wouldn't eat *anything*. At least he looked nice enough now that he was clean and freshly dressed in his khakis and smartly striped t-shirt.

The doorbell rang as she was putting on his shoes. "Shit!" Dillon exclaimed happily.

"Oh God," said Carol, wondering if this was the only thing Dillon was going to pick up from his visit here. She hoped he'd said it before. Maybe his mother had said it? Or that woman who babysat for her? Carol could blame it on her. "Goodness," she could say. "Where did he pick up such language?" Or was that too stilted? Was that a suspicious thing to say?

You're one golly-gee away from sounding like one of the Youngmans, Carol.

Carol answered the door distractedly, forgetting to look through the peephole. "Shit, shit, shit," she could hear Dillon intoning behind her, which echoed her thoughts perfectly when the door swung open and the man on the porch said, "Hello."

It was Graham.

Because of course it was.

"Yes?" she said brusquely.

"Hi," he said, instead of answering, looking down at Dillon, who had come over to lean against Carol's leg and look up at the visitor. "What's your name?"

"It's Dillon," Carol answered. She was annoyed with Graham for asking and being here and for being nice to Dillon, because that made it harder to be rude to him. "What did you need?"

"Well, I noticed the little guy visiting, so I brought over some toys I had around the house. I thought maybe you could use them. You can bring them back after your guest leaves."

Spying again! She had been wondering what was in the box he was carrying.

"He's only been here since this morning. Do you have me under surveillance?"

Graham looked really hurt by this and Carol regretted saying it, but now that it was out, she saw no way to backpedal it. It had been harsh, but she'd meant every word. Every time the man opened those curtains of his, it was like he was making the whole street his business.

He put the box down on the porch and stepped back. "Look, I'll just leave these here. If you don't want them, just set them on my porch. You don't need to ring the bell or anything." He said this very firmly, obviously angry. "It was nice to meet you, Dillon."

Screw you, Carol, hovered in the air, unspoken.

He turned, tight-faced, spinning rapidly away as he marched down the walkway.

Carol closed the door without picking up the box and watched Graham's slightly stoop-shouldered back through the peephole as he walked up to his house. He didn't look back. Why would he? He had been kind. So he had noticed the boy—that didn't necessarily mean he was spying on her. Even if he did like looking out his window, he looked at everyone. Like that guy in *Rear Window.* And she had taken it personally. Now she looked like a vindictive bitch.

Carol leaned her head against the door and cried, as all her stress broke upon her like cresting waves. Why had she been so mean? Why couldn't anything just go right, for *once*?

She went to the stairs and sat down and put her head on her arms and sobbed. A few minutes later, Dillon came up and put his little arms around her. He began to cry, too.

That made her feel worse.

"Oh, Dillon. Honey, it's all right. Really. See? I'm not crying anymore."

She wiped her cheeks with the back of her hand. Even though she felt horrible at upsetting the boy, part of her—a seemingly non-irrational part, was telling her to enjoy this emotional congruence with the boy. And so rather than feeling completely sad, she felt sad and touched and happy in some strange, obscurely maternal way that he actually cared what she felt and thought, which was tinged with the knowledge that Dillon was not hers and never would be, and that soon she would be back to being completely alone, with no one to care about her feelings at all.

The thought nearly made her cry all over again. Even though part of her had been eager to go back to her pre-Dillon life, of order cleanliness, and quiet, he had sliced through the sterilized whiteness of her life like a brightly colored knife. All these conflicted feelings in her head jangled like bits of shattered mirror now, each reflecting a bit of her soul, but no part captured the whole picture of herself that always remained just out of sight, like the blind spot in a human eye.

Dillon stopped crying and so did Carol. She gave him a last little hug and stood up. "Let's go to the store," she said, smiling down at Dillon who was now pulling at a string from the inside hem of his shirt. He allowed her to take his free hand and the two of them went to the door.

As they left, Carol carefully moved the box from Graham from the porch to the hall.

■□■□■□■

The store was a success. Dillon loved looking at the food. He liked squeezing the bread. He squeezed her poor loaf of sourdough so enthusiastically that Carol was tempted to put it back and get a new one. But she didn't, because she was afraid that someone might see.

She learned that one should never park a child close to a bin of apples when she turned her back, only to see a cascade of them go rolling by in the corner of her eye, with Dillon holding one in his chubby fist. Then she tried to help pick up the avalanche of Granny Smiths dislodged by Dillon, who had apparently chosen one of the key supports for what seemed like hundreds of apples. The produce manager shooed her away, saying it happened all the time. Carol was pretty sure that was a lie, but it was a kind lie. Probably because he was a kind man, which made her feel guilty, because when she had walked in, she had thought his mustache reminded her of Hitler's.

Not for the first time, Carol was conscious of being grateful that people couldn't read minds. Particularly hers. Telepathy would have been the most intrusive burden. She would have to watch every single unkind thought that gravitated through her consciousness like shavings of iron to a very powerful magnet.

Telepathy had featured in Graham's sci-fi novel, the one he had given her. She couldn't remember the exact plot, only that some of the women had been telepaths and the men had not. It had struck Carol as very paranoid and possibly sexist. She had inferred that Graham distrusted women and spent what was probably far too much time obsessing over what women had thought about him, and then turning it into filth, like Robert Heinlein.

But now, as she thought about it, perhaps women had only been a device to explore the issue. In which case, that was yet another thought she was grateful that no one would ever see. *Sometimes*, she told herself, *a mustache is just a mustache, and a psychic is just a psychic.*

Having made her escape from the apple fiasco, Carol found herself in the frozen food aisle. Dillon was in heaven. He liked reaching for the handles of the doors on the frozen food cases, opening them and then slamming them shut. Carol bought lots of frozen pizzas remembering

Melinda's assurance that Dillon would eat them. She also tried to ignore Dillon and the doors. Other women in the frozen food aisle did not and some of them frowned at Carol, as if wondering why she wasn't putting a stop to things. Carol ignored them, too. It was easier than she would have imagined. Perhaps Dillon, with his uncommunicativeness, was on to something.

As she shopped, she kept up a running commentary for Dillon's benefit regarding the food she was picking out. Sometimes she read the ingredients to him, and that took up virtually all her attention and made it even easier to tune out the whispers and the glares.

Dillon, completely mesmerized by the freezer doors, ignored her.

As she was rounding the corner of the frozen food aisles to checkout, she felt a tap on her shoulder. She turned to find an older gentleman looking at her with an intense combination of what she thought looked like embarrassment and friendliness.

"Excuse me," he began.

"Yes?" Carol said warily, giving the man what she hoped was a confident smile. Was he going to lecture her about Dillon's behavior? Or perhaps he needed help getting something from a shelf—

"Um, your boy there. He's sprung a leak." The man pointed to a trail of droplets trailing around the corner of the aisle she'd just come from.

"Oh God. Oh no. Thanks for telling me." Shit. That explained the looks and whispers. What should she do? She asked the man if he would stand with Dillon, not even pausing to consider whether or not he was a child molester in her panic. That fear came to her as she was speaking to a box girl and appraising her of the situation, and this new fear added a desperate quaver to her voice that made the girl put down the box cutter and lead her to a kiosk with a built-in trash can and storage cupboard, from which she produced a roll of thick brown towels.

"Here," she said. "You'll need these."

No offer of help was forthcoming. Carol was annoyed. Isn't that what these employees were paid for? But she was too focused on returning to Dillon to linger on her irritation. Luckily, the man hadn't absconded with him, and he left quickly as soon as Carol brought out the paper towels, as if he feared he might be conscripted to assist in this, too.

Carol made a huge wad of towels and shoved them under Dillon's soaking butt. She looked at the trail of pee on the floor but she didn't have enough towels to wipe down the whole aisle, not after the wad she'd nested under Dillon. And she had brought no diapers with her.

How optimistic—and foolish.

She swung the car to the personal hygiene aisle and grabbed a huge bag of XL disposables. Then she and Dillon wound their way to the check stand, accidentally ending up in the 15 items or less line. (At least it wasn't the 9 items or less/cash only line, she thought desperately.) The checker and all the people behind her had been too polite to say anything, but not too polite to give her looks. Once, she had been the one giving those looks to the harried people who wound up in front of her in the express line, tapping her foot at those old people writing traveler's checks and distracted mothers with screaming children, silently cursing them because she had assumed that they were cheating the system on purpose.

It was at this most inopportune of moments that Carol happened to see Ray Flock standing towards the end of the express line. The same line she was currently holding up. He was juggling a six-pack of beer and an armload of Hungry-Man frozen dinners.

"Paper or plastic?" asked the bagger.

"Whatever," Carol said quietly, hoping Ray had not seen her or recognized her voice. She turned her head, hoping that she looked like just another anonymous woman.

"What?" the bagger spoke very loudly.

"Paper," said Carol, in a slightly strangled voice.

The bagger sighed. She had obviously disappointed him. Clearly the correct choice was plastic. Better to fill a landfill than to kill a tree. All right-thinking customers (who also used the express lane correctly) probably chose plastic. Each snap of the paper bag seemed like a recrimination. Carol hoped her face was not quite as red as it felt.

Dillon, meanwhile, had fallen asleep with his face mashed against the cart.

"Do you want help out?" asked the bagger.

Of course she wanted help. But not his help. She could tell he was praying she said no. She was tempted to say yes just to be completely annoying, but somehow, she just couldn't do it.

"No, thank you," whispered Carol, darting a nervous look at Ray.

And then she was off, receipt in hand. She had escaped. She was free.

She decided she would not go out again with Dillon. She had apparently not graduated to public child care. She might be adequate at home (and if she wasn't, at least no one was around to witness the failure), but in public spaces, failure could be spectacular.

Carol loaded up the trunk of her car with groceries and began to lift Dillon out of the shopping cart. Pee drizzled lazily down his sodden legs. Well, that was disgusting.

She stripped him behind the open door of the car and put all his clothes and his diaper in her travel waste basket, which until now, had mostly just held Diet Coke cans and candy wrappers. Dillon, she put in one of the new diapers before lining his car seat with what remained of the paper towels she had accidentally carried out with her. Just as she was fastening the buckle, she heard Ray's familiar voice echo through the parking lot.

"Hey there, Carol. I thought that was you."

She cracked her head on the roof of the car as she backed herself out. *Damn it.*

"Hi, Ray. I didn't see you there." *Liar.* "Were you shopping?"

How stupid. He was carrying a bag of groceries. Could she have said anything more idiotic?

"Just a few things," said Ray. "So who's the kid?"

"I'm just baby-sitting for a friend. It's been a nightmare so far. I'm not very experienced around kids." Should she have said that? Didn't men love women who were naturally good around kids? Was she somehow admitting to being an inferior sort of woman?

"Maybe I'll drop by and give you a hand. I've had plenty of experience." Ray was edging back now, clearly ready to be off. Carol wondered if he regretted stopping to talk, if he realized how insincere his offer sounded.

"I'd love that. I'm sure Dillon would, too. That would be great. Great . . ." Carol spoke brightly. Too brightly. Jesus, she sounded desperate. She was oozing desperation.

"Well," said Ray. "I guess I'll see you later."

"Nice to see you," called Carol. Again, too brightly, she thought.

All the way home, accompanied by the flighty strains of Joni Mitchell's "Car on a Hill," Carol obsessed over how unfair life was. When you wanted to meet someone and you were ready to meet them, at your best and dressed to the nines, the person you wanted to see was nowhere to be seen. But as soon as you forgot to shave your legs or put on makeup or wash your hair or tweeze your chin—or if you were holding a pee-soaked wad of paper towels—there *they* were, looking at your sorry excuse of a self and clearly regretting their acquaintance with you.

Carol marched Dillon right up to the bath as soon as they got home. She left him in the tub while she started his wet clothes in the laundry, along with his park clothes. She almost forgot to bring in the food from the car, and remembered only as she was washing her hands.

There was a message on her answering machine. Her heart leaped when she thought it might be from Melinda, but it was from Officer Muller. He wanted her to know that a suspect had been apprehended in the murder of her husband. Gerald had been hit by a drunk driver with a suspended license. Officer Muller went on to extend his condolences and to thank her for her help. He left his phone number. Why? Was he hitting on her?

She realized that she had almost completely forgotten about Gerald today. Poor Gerald, he had just evaporated, like a mediocre dream. Not even a bad dream, just one she hardly remembered. Could you really waste your whole life that way? Would she and Gerald have spent their whole lives in some sort of purgatorial fugue if he hadn't been killed?

Of course, Gerald had told Melinda that he had been planning to be with her. But had he been? She hadn't seen any evidence of that. He hadn't been cleaning out his stuff or packing up important things or moving money around. *And there were certainly no pretty blue boxes from Tiffany*, she thought wryly. There was nothing. Not a trace of his intentions. Of course, maybe what had been purgatory for her hadn't been for Gerald. Maybe his plan had been to string Melinda along and keep her obliviously running to the dry cleaners with his suits and putting meals on the table.

It made her head ache to think about Gerald and Melinda and herself. Mostly, it made her head ache to think about herself, period. She felt as if her life with Gerald had been a sinkhole into which all her dreams and purpose and lifeforce had slowly been falling without a trace, and without her awareness that it was even happening. And now, not even a visible hole was left as evidence.

She had bought too much food to fit into the freezers. She stuffed the one in the house full and then tried to cram the rest into the freezer in the garage, but there had been more in it than she thought. Things she had bought with and for Gerald and herself. She decided to throw out some mysterious bags of brown meat strips. They were a whitish brown and badly freezer burned. She also found another mystery bag with fish in it, but at least this one was dated. It was from the 80s.

Finally, she had enough space to jam in Dillon's pizzas. If she really pushed down on them, she could make them all fit. She went back to check on Dillon in the bath, half-filled with a nameless, wordless panic that something would be wrong. She found him playing happily.

"Let's get into PJs, Dillon," she said, letting the water out of the tub. She dried him off. He smelled sweet and soapy and was beginning to yawn, which she took as a good sign.

They dined on pizza and milk and sliced apples for dinner. The apples reminded Carol of the disaster in the produce aisle, which led to thoughts of the leaking diaper, which in turn led to thoughts about Ray. Carol felt mortified all over again. She hoped Melinda was not having a good time. She was extremely annoyed with Melinda.

Putting Dillon to bed was lovely, though. Carol sat in a chair by his bed and read him a story from a book that she'd had since she was a little girl, which she had found in the bottom of her cedar hope chest along with a scrap of her own blankie—her own Baba, she thought—and Mr. Fuzzums, her old white bear. The book was a rhyming book with a picture of the ocean in the front, done in vivid early 60s colors. Now, people would probably call it psychedelic or retro, but back then it had just been normal. A small boat with a white sail was visible far out on the turquoise waves. The beach was littered with sand dollars and shells and a little red crab was scuttling across the yellow sand towards a piece of driftwood. Dillon ran his fingers over the picture. He seemed to especially like the seagull.

"I had a little boat." Carol pointed to the boat.

"I took it to the sea. I played with my boat." Carol turned the page so Dillon could see the little boy in the picture tenderly putting his little boat in the water. "But it sailed away from me." She pointed to the picture of the little boat sailing away into a huge wide ocean that engulfed it.

"The waves brought in seaweed." Carol turned the page towards Dillon that showed brown and green seaweed lying over the sandy beach. The little crab seemed to be watching everything from where he peered out under his driftwood. "The waves brought in foam." Here was a picture of crashing blue waves and white foam. "But the waves never did bring my little boat back home."

The last picture was a sunset across a wide and smooth expanse of darkening ocean and the little boat was sailing away towards the sunset, its tiny white sail colored pink and orange, reflecting the hues of the sky. Carol decided it was a much sadder story than she remembered but Dillon hadn't heard the end. He was asleep. When Carol bent to kiss his cheek, he sighed softly.

Although it was only 8pm, Carol decided to go to bed, too. She was exhausted. This was turning out to be a lot more work than she expected. *I knew there was a reason I didn't have kids*, she thought, staring up at the ceiling. But for some reason, this thought made her sad, too.

When Carol woke up, she felt like she had been dreaming for weeks.

Then she remembered Dillon.

She went in to check on him and found him curled in the fetal position, wrapped only in a sheet. The light cotton blanket, as well as the quilt and his pillow, were in a heap at the foot of his bed.

Carol sat in the chair where she had read to him last night and watched him sleep. A little puddle of drool had wet the sheet under his bed. She reached out to run her hand across his forehead. *What a good boy you are*, she thought, a little sadly.

Sighing, she went downstairs to put the coffee on. She had always loved the smell more than she did the taste. At this point, brewing it was habit, like everything else she did in this house.

She went out to get the paper while the coffee finished and saw that Gerald's hit-and-run driver had made the front page, bottom-right corner. A small article, but big enough to be seen by all the neighbors. Especially neighbors named Graham.

Carol threw the paper into the trash without reading it. And then she wondered if she should have gone to Kinko's and made copies of the clipping to send to Gerald's family. But since they hadn't bothered contacting her, she didn't feel like going through the effort.

Not when it was all she could do to keep herself moving and hold herself together.

Dillon padded downstairs a few minutes after the coffee was ready. Carol, remembering the diaper incident from yesterday, changed him immediately. She tried to entice Dillon to use the potty, maybe even to just sit on it, but he wasn't at all interested. His new underwear were sitting on the back of the tank but apparently they weren't as interesting to him now as they had been in the store. He completely ignored them, as he ignored so much else.

Oh well. Toilet training was really Melinda's problem anyway.

After breakfast, she pulled out the box of toys that Graham had brought over for Dillon.

There was a train set made out of light-colored wood with brightly-colored train cars held together by little magnets. There were green wooden trees glossy with paint, and little block houses that had bright red roofs. It was a very cheery little train set and looked old. Maybe as old as her picture book was. Carol wondered if it had been Graham's when he was a child.

As with Gerald, it was hard to imagine Graham as a child. All she could imagine was a miniature version of Graham: stoop-shouldered, graying, and thin. She could imagine him small, yes, but she could not imagine him young.

Maybe that was just the way it went when you got older.

Dillon tried to put the track together but the tongue and groove construction of the track was hard for him to manage. And Carol was afraid that Dillon might damage the wood if he pounded on it, so she put the track together herself and let Dillon put out all the pieces, watching amusedly as Dillon lined up all the trees in a single row on one of the railroad tracks.

"Dillon, trees don't grow on the railroad track. That's silly."

Dillon looked at Carol and back at the trees. But he didn't move the trees and she didn't, either.

"Let's see what else is in the box, okay?"

Dillon drove the train into the trees with an "RRRRR" while Carol opened up a blue bag with a red cord that had "My Building Blocks" embroidered on it in white letters. Inside were multicolored wooden blocks: blue squares, red rectangles, purple columns, orange triangles, yellow arches, and little green half moons that fit perfectly inside the carved-out spaces of the yellow pieces.

Together, Carol and Dillon built a village across the white carpet of the living room floor, and to her surprise, she actually found that she was enjoying herself quite a bit.

"You know, Dillon," Carol said, after about an hour of watching Dillon mow down buildings and trees with the train car, "we should go across the street and thank Mr. Sterling for these toys. What do you think?"

Dillon ran the train car back and forth across the carpet.

"Well, I say we should." She stood up too fast and felt a bit dizzy. Her knees were throbbing a little from all that time on the floor. She was not looking forward to apologizing to Graham but she needed to do it now before she lost her resolve and let things become too weird.

She and Dillon walked across the street. The house gleamed in the sunny glare of the late morning. The trees weren't big enough yet to shade the houses or the street and Carol could feel the sun reflecting off those huge stucco homes. Dillon tripped on the curb that fronted Graham's house and Carol bent to him, but despite his skinned knee, he didn't seem very bothered by it.

"Do you have an owie, Dillon?"

He ignored her and picked at his hem.

All right then. Carol pushed the doorbell. She could hear the chimes in Graham's hall, as if in some big gothic castle, and then she saw a shadow moving through the frosted glass. The shadow paused, and for a few minutes, Carol wondered if he was just going to wait there with the door closed and just never speak to her again.

Idiot, you don't even like him.

The door opened a crack.

"Yes?" said Graham, looking at her with an expression she could not identify. He was wearing a V-neck shirt and jeans, but his feet were bare. He had very nice feet, she couldn't help but noticing. Gerald had had hairy toes, and bunions that came from his fine Italian shoes.

Graham's, she couldn't help but notice, were finely arched with long, even toes.

"Hi," said Carol. The overly bright voice was back. Shit. "I came to say I'm sorry."

She looked down again, this time at his floor, tiled in what looked like slate. Graham was silent. Dillon was humming softly.

"I didn't mean to snap at you," she continued. "I know you're not really looking at me—I mean, spying on me. I know that, and I'm really sorry I said what I said. I've been a little off lately because—well, you know why—and I hope you can forgive me. I wouldn't, um. I don't know if I could forgive me, if I were you."

Graham was still silent.

"I don't usually act this way," she continued lamely. "Or maybe I do, but I certainly don't mean for it to come out the way it does and then, well, if I say any more I might just make it worse, so I had better stop here." She spread out her hands as if hoping that lightning would strike her dead and end her misery here, between Graham's two neatly pruned fig trees.

"Anyway, that's what I wanted to say. Thanks for the toys, those were great, too. We're really enjoying them." God, she should have just written a note and slipped it into the mailbox like a normal person instead of ambushing him at the door like a madwoman.

"Well, I didn't expect this," Graham said at length. "I'm sorry, I'd invite you in but this isn't a good time. I understand, I really do. Don't worry about it. In fact, I'd like to take you and Dillon out somewhere when I can free up the time."

"Dillon isn't going to be around much longer." When Graham's eyebrows shot up, she added hastily, "His mom picks him up on Sunday. But thanks for the offer. That's really nice. And you've been very gracious about my apology. Thanks for that, too. You made it easier than I, uh, than I thought it was going to be."

What a lie that is, she thought. *Nothing ever makes groveling apologies easy.*

"Well then, Dillon, I hope maybe you'll come visit some other time."

Graham extended his hand to Dillon. Dillon looked at the hand expectantly, and then in Carol's general direction, and then back at the hand. He waited.

Carol laughed. "I think he thinks you're going to give him something. I don't think he knows about shaking hands."

Graham went down on one knee and took Dillon's small right hand, folding it into his own large one, and gently pumped Dillon's arm up and down.

Dillon looked puzzled and Graham smiled. "You'll get used to it." To Carol, he said, "Thanks for coming over. It was a big thing to do."

Was it? She stared at him, a little dazed. She had never noticed before that Graham was actually a fairly good-looking man. She had been too annoyed with him to take in the good bone structure, the long thin nose, the dark brows, the good skin that had very few wrinkles except around his greenish eyes. Yes, he really was quite nice to look at. Not in the muscular compact way of the Rays of the world, but slender and slouching, like a rakish count.

Interesting, she thought, and then shook herself off. *No more BBC.*

"Bye!" she said again, before picking up Dillon's hand for the walk home. "Mommy comes back on Sunday, Dillon. Won't that be nice?"

Dillon looked at her, or perhaps past her, without much enthusiasm. That was somewhat gratifying. Maybe she was better with kids than she thought.

Or maybe Melinda was an awful mother. She felt a little guilty for that thought until she remembered the way that Dillon had cowered back from her in the Target, and then her heart hardened. She wondered if she should make an anonymous report somewhere. But to whom and what kind of report? And based on what proof?

They drove through Burger Boys for burgers, fries, and shakes for dinner. Carol was too tired to make anything. Dillon ate an amazing amount of his dinner. Junk food was clearly his favorite. He licked every one of his French fries and then mashed them up into little balls, which he then ate. The burger he took apart layer by layer, eating each piece separately, except for the tomato. Dillon put the tomato off to the side and poked at it every now and then, as if checking its pulse.

"The wild tomato is a dangerous vegetable," Carol said, faking Steve Irwin's accent when Dillon went in to poke at the tomato again. He didn't look up. Carol sighed.

After dinner, they went to the living room and played with Graham's train set and blocks until Dillon fell asleep next to his train around 7pm. Carol let him sleep, which proved to be unwise when he was awake and ready for action at 9pm. But since Melinda was coming back on Sunday anyway, Carol figured she'd have plenty of time to catch up on her rest. She was on bereavement leave, after all. What else was she going to do?

So she turned on the TV and watched *The Wolfman* with Dillon from ten to midnight. At first she was worried he might think it would be too scary, but he fell asleep on Carol's lap before the movie even ended.

She picked him up and took him back to his bed at midnight. She tucked him in and kissed him goodnight before returning to the master bedroom to go to sleep.

C arol was awakened by what she thought was a crash. She lifted her head off the pillow and listened, and only heard silence. She was tired. She wanted to go back to sleep. Probably, she had just imagined the noise. She put her head back on the pillow and closed her eyes, and was just beginning to drift off again when she heard Dillon cry.

Instantly, she was awake. *Oh shit.*

His bedroom, when she got to it, was empty, and she did not immediately know where he was. Then, as she hurried down the stairs, she found him sitting on one of the steps with his head stuck in the railings. He had his two hands on either side of his head and he was pushing with all his might against the railings that had trapped his head, red-faced and sobbing.

"Dillon, how did you *do* this?" she asked, as if he was going to answer her. "Dillon, this was very naughty. Very, very bad, Dillon."

Dillon continued to cry and struggle.

Yes, that's it. Yell at the boy. That will get his head unstuck.

Graham's train lay on the tile below the stairs where Dillon was trapped. That must have been the crash she'd heard. He must have stuck his head through the rails to look down at it or else he'd been trying to go through the balcony in order to go after it. Oh God, she hoped not.

Apparently stairs were yet another death trap she hadn't thought to baby-proof.

Carol tried twisting Dillon's head. His ears seemed to be the main problem in retracting his head. But when she tried to pull, he squirmed and let out a yelp.

She picked the kicking Dillon up and turned him sideways until his ears popped loose, and then she gently eased him out. He looked fine, she thought with relief, although his ears were quite red.

She put him down immediately, rubbing at her shoulders. Her muscles were already aching and her knee was protesting the extended kneel, especially after yesterday's floor playing. Lifting small boys was something her body was not quite used to. Maybe if she'd actually made more of an effort at the gym, she thought ruefully.

"Come on, Dillon. Let's go out to breakfast." She no longer felt like cooking.

She put Dillon into some shorts and a t-shirt, after changing his wet nighttime diaper. Then after pulling on some high-waisted jeans and a t-shirt herself, she got Dillon strapped into his car seat.

They went to the Blue Bee Eatery. Carol had butter pecan pancakes and she ordered strawberry waffles for Dillon, thinking that he might enjoy them after the way he'd sucked down his strawberry shake from the other night. She was amazed at its size when it came. It was covered with whip cream and looked more like a dessert than a breakfast.

Dillon immediately bent his head and licked up the whip cream.

"Silverware, honey," Carol said nervously. "Use the silverware."

Lick. Lick. Lick.

"Dillon!"

Dillon looked up at Carol. She noticed he didn't actually look right at her. His eyes sort of made a dance around her while looking in her general direction. She held his face and tried to look into his eyes. The eyes immediately scooted off into another direction.

"Dillon," she said. "I'm over here."

She waved her hand in front of him. His eyes were now looking out to the extreme right of the room. Fine, then. She picked up the spoon and waved it in front of where the eyes were focusing, before gently putting it into his hand and curling his fingers around it.

"Eat with your spoon."

Dillon seemed to understand. He shoveled the spoon into the whip cream and began to lick the spoon. Carol decided she could live with that.

After breakfast, they drove around for a while. She took a backroad that went by a tennis club and into the hills. They drove by small ranches and pastures filled with cows and sheep and alpacas. Carol pointed out all the animals she saw, naming them. "Look Dillon, a cow! Mooo, moooo. Look, Dillon, over there—it's a sheep! What do the sheep say, Dillon? Baa, baaa." She wasn't exactly sure what sounds an alpaca made, so she skipped over those.

Dillon never answered, which made her feel a little silly. She wasn't even sure if he was looking at the animals she was pointing out, or if he was off in his own little world, but she did it until Dillon fell asleep. Carol was actually reluctant to drive home. She was quite enjoying the sunny day, the empty road, the occasional glimpse of deer and quail. But she needed to take care of the Goodwill donations and Maria was coming in the afternoon. She didn't like Maria to see her disorganized. She always liked to clean up the bathrooms a bit before Maria came, too, and empty the trash. The idea of having "hired help" vaguely embarrassed Carol and she didn't want Maria to think that she was a lazy, entitled snob.

Carol left Dillon asleep in the car while she loaded the Goodwill bags filled with Gerald's things into the front seat. She couldn't remember what time the store opened or where the delivery station was, but she thought she might have seen one of the blue and white trucks behind the Safeway, once.

The man running the station was wearing a Bill Cosby-like sweater and dirt-covered jeans. He had on heavy black boots and hadn't shaved. He came down the ladder from inside the truck where he had been sitting as he sorted through boxes and walked over without greeting her.

He didn't speak as she got the bags out of the car. He just stood there and watched before heaving them into the truck and then he prepared to go back up the stairs as soon as she was done.

"Can I have a receipt?" Carol asked.

The man looked at her with his very pale blue eyes. They seemed to have a white haze over them. He grabbed a clipboard and thrust it at her. *Okay then*, thought Carol.

She filled out the form and he tore off the donor copy, shoving it at her, before crumpling up the store copy into his pocket. She put the clipboard, which he had left her holding, back on the bed of the truck. The man had already returned to his station and left the clipboard lying there in the sun. "Thanks," said Carol, wincing. It came out sounding a little sarcastic.

The man said nothing. He just stared at her. Carol remembered when she was a little girl there had been a man who stared like that who had lived on her street. Every day, walking home, she would hope he wouldn't be there, but of course, he always was. Sometimes she would cross to the other side of the street. Occasionally, she would walk the long way around the block so she didn't have to go by his house. She thought, in her childlike fear and egocentrism, that he was waiting there for *her*. He used to sit in an old wicker chair, she remembered that. And the lawn in front of his house had been high with weeds. It used to give her father fits when they'd drive by. "Driving the prices down!" he would exclaim, as they drove by, but that was the 50s when a man judged another man by the caliber of his lawn and simply being Catholic could be enough to make people look at you funny.

Thank goodness things are better now, she thought. But then she wondered: were they? She thought of how casually Diana had judged Dillon, and how casually Melinda seemed to judge her. Maybe society just went on judging and judging itself, and it was only the *how* that changed. Wasn't that just a depressing thought?

Dillon was still asleep when they got home. Carol woke him by getting him out of the car seat. She let him run around on the grass for a while and then she wondered if there was any chance Melinda might come home early and see her boy looking so bright and happy in the sun.

Melinda didn't come, and after a while, Carol brought Dillon back in, not wanting him to get sunburned. She tried to find some cartoons for him on the TV but most of them seemed to be on early in the morning. Later in the day, there wasn't much for kids to watch except on the premium channels. She and Gerald hadn't watched much TV so they had never had more than basic cable. There was a documentary about trains that briefly captured his attention, but then he got bored and started shaking the legs of her low table so violently that Carol was afraid he'd knock things off.

To distract him, she got out the train set and blocks, and she and Dillon spent the next few hours playing some more with Graham's toys. She read to Dillon from another book she had found, but half the time, he didn't seem to be listening at all.

Finally, Maria came and offered to take Dillon for a walk after she finished cleaning. "You rest," she said. It was a command Carol was only too happy to obey.

She lay down fully dressed and shut her eyes. She had to think of something to do with Dillon tomorrow. The beach or the zoo. She couldn't decide which. Maybe she would ask Maria, she thought sleepily. Maria would know best.

She awoke to Maria gently tapping her on the back. It was 5:45, Carol saw, when she leaned over to look at the clock. She'd been asleep for two hours."

"Oh! Maria! I'm so sorry. I didn't realize—"

"You look so tired, I let you sleep. I fed Dillon and made tea. He's playing. You know there is something wrong with that little boy."

So I've been told, Carol thought grimly.

"But he very sweet," Maria added, conciliatory.

"Maria, I left your envelope on the kitchen table, like always."

Maria patted her purse. She had already picked it up.

"Great. Well. See you next week, then."

In the other room, Carol could hear Maria saying goodbye to Dillon. When she got to the foyer, she noticed Dillon didn't even watch as Maria went out the door. He was completely absorbed in the task of rolling his train back and forth.

Shit. Carol realized she had forgotten to ask Maria whether she should go to the zoo or the beach. She didn't want to delay her any more than she already had by asking now.

She watched out the window as Maria got into her little brown Toyota. Now she would have to make the decision alone. All the responsibility was on her. She felt like crying.

She wondered how Melinda managed. Not very well, probably.

Carol tried to put Dillon to bed early. He didn't want to go. She read to him until she got hoarse, resorting to the *Birds of America* book in her desperation, and then asked him, "Tomorrow, Dillon, beach or zoo?"

He looked at her blankly.

"Beach or zoo?" She made the whooshing sound of ocean waves and the chittering of a monkey.

"Shit," said Dillon.

Carol nodded. Indeed.

She patted his head and turned the light down as far as it could go so that there was only a faint orange glow. She wasn't sure if he was afraid of the dark. Probably, she thought. The ceiling lamp made a faint ringing nose when she did this, which Dillon seemed to like or didn't mind.

She went to her room and thought about taking a bath. Usually, being in her lavishly decorated bathroom cheered her, but she couldn't hear things very well in the bathroom and liked being able to hear what Dillon was up to, especially after the incident with the stairs. Quick showers were her best friends, now.

She lay in bed, in the dark, and wondered what life was like for Dillon at home. She had no idea whether he was enrolled in preschool, or if he had any friends, or what he did all day.

Melinda had mentioned the neighbor who watched him. She wondered if Gerald had ever been active in raising him. It certainly would have explained why he had quit talking about children. Dillon was enough to put a reluctant parent off children forever, she thought. Not that he didn't have his good qualities. But Gerald had never been the type of person to be won over by smiles and goofs.

Maybe if he had been, their relationship wouldn't have deteriorated the way it had.

SATURDAY APRIL 27, 1992

Carol opened her eyes to the steady thrum of rain. She could also hear the trickle of water running in the gutter that threaded along the roof above the master bedroom window. She shoved the curtains aside to look outside. The valley of Agua Verde was swaddled in a gray blanket of rain. She could see the rain splashing in the pool, the haze of clouds obscuring the buildings in the distance. It looked like it must have been raining most of the night, everything was so saturated.

No zoo, then. Or beach.

She went to check in on Dillon. He wasn't in bed, of course.

She went downstairs. No Dillon.

She checked the lock on the front door—still locked, which meant he was in the house somewhere. Unless he had gone out the back door and drowned in the pool. Nope, she checked that, too. Still locked.

Why does this keep happening? she thought, padding back into the guest room.

Dillon's new clothes were hanging on the rail in the closet and there were a few boxes in the corner, but nothing that could hide a small boy. Then she heard a very faint rustling that seemed to be coming from the bed. Carol got down on her hands and knees—*ugh, again?*—and looked underneath the bed.

There was Dillon, curled up and sleeping beneath the mattress. He was lying on some papers that had been stacked under there and must have shifted to create the noise she'd heard.

He woke up as she began to reel him out like a hooked fish. And then he kicked at her and crawled out the rest of the way himself with Baba in one clenched fist.

"Why, Dillon?" Carol asked wearily.

"Wah," said Dillon, chewing on Baba.

It was still raining when they went downstairs but at least now there were Saturday morning cartoons. Jim Henson's *Dog City, Bobby's World, Tom and Jerry Kids.* Dillon seemed to love them. He sat, rapt, in front of the large screen TV, giggling occasionally.

Carol put on the radio. Annie Lennox was playing and the brooding sound of her voice went well with the slight gloominess brought on by the rain. Keeping it low so it wouldn't disturb Dillon's program, Carol began to make her coffee.

When the cartoons ended, Dillon came and found her in the kitchen while she was chopping up apples as the eggs sizzled in their pan. He began to open and close all the kitchen cabinets until she shooed him away for getting too close to the stove. Then he began to empty them out, one by one. Carol let him since that seemed harmless, even though it meant stepping over saucepans and stewpots, though she frustrated him by not letting him play in the Corningware cupboard because the Corningware was breakable—and expensive.

Dillon banged a pot and lid together and looked at her feet pointedly after she told him "no" for the fifth time. Finally, she sat in the kitchen chair she had put in front of the Corningware cupboard to prevent Dillon from gaining access. She tried to entice him with the fruit and eggs. Dillon did not want the fruit and eggs. Dillon wanted to bang the pot he was holding louder. When he got no response, he started slamming the steel lid and pan into the wooden cabinets.

Carol hastily set down her bowl of food. "No! No, Dillon!"

Carol wrenched both pot and lid out of his hands.

Dillon immediately became a little ball and covered his head with his hands.

Carol hugged him and felt him shudder.

"Dillon, I'm not going to hurt you." She stroked his hair. No response. "Dillon, it's okay, really it is. I just don't want you banging the pot into my cupboards. But I'm not really mad. Look at me, Dillon. I'm not mad at you."

Dillon slowly uncovered his head but he still wouldn't look at her.

Carol gave him back the pot and lid. She banged them together, with their hands joined, and said, "Yes!!!" which earned her a wavery little smile that nearly broke her heart.

Then she made a motion to hit the cupboard with the pot lid and said, "No, no, no—okay?"

Dillon banged the pot and lid together, drowning out the radio. He played with the pot and lid for what seemed like hours, too distracted to eat his meal. Carol began to worry about his hearing and hers. It was about the time that Carol began wondering whether she should risk another confrontation by taking his pot and lid away when he discovered the silverware drawer.

He immediately tossed both pot and lid aside and started taking out the spoons. For a moment, he held all of them in his hands like a gleaming metal bouquet. Then, almost in slow motion, he opened his hands and the spoons fell in a bright arc around him. Dillon let out a little shriek. Carol's first impression was that he was scared, but when he gathered them all up again to repeat the procedure, she realized she had been mistaken. He was delighted. Very, very delighted.

Again and again, Carol watched Dillon drop the spoons.

Was this as irritating as the pan/lid action? No, she thought. Not quite.

Eventually, he got hungry enough to abandon the spoons on the floor and eat his now cold and rubbery eggs. They took a rain walk under a big rainbow umbrella, big enough for two, that she and Gerald had never used. They stopped to look at a creek covered in algae, teeming with small tadpoles. "Weh," said Dillon, and Carol said, "Yes, Dillon. Wet."

To ensure success, Carol made pizza as an early dinner.

While the pizza was cooking, Dillon discovered the oven light. On and off. On and off. Suddenly, Dillon turned to Carol and said, "Hummy."

"What?" said Carol, surprised.

"Hummy," repeated Dillon. "Hummy." He paused. "I hummy."

"You're hungry, Dillon?" she said breathlessly. "Hungry?" She rubbed her tummy and then his, delighted when he covered his face and nodded.

After dinner, Dillon played on the swivel chair in Gerald's office—no, *her* office—while she went through her desk, trying to figure out what she needed to keep and what to throw out. She made a pile that was definitely trash and a pile for papers that looked important.

She kept expecting to find some trace of Melinda in the desk. Some hint of Gerald's clandestine other life—a photo, a necklace, *something*. But there was no hint of a personal life at all in the desk. It was as if Gerald hadn't really existed here as a person with a life of any kind, other than his work.

Carol wasn't sure why this surprised her, but it did. He hadn't known how to be anyone but himself, so why did she expect that he would be different with anyone else?

Dillon was falling asleep in the chair so Carol carried him up the stairs. He was much heavier than she remembered. Or maybe she was just getting weaker after spending four days with him.

Carol went to bed and set the alarm for 6am. Melinda might be back early and she wanted to have him fed and clean and packed with all of his new things. She slipped on cotton shorts and a t-shirt and fell right to sleep without any dreams that she could remember.

Carol woke up half an hour earlier than the alarm. The sky was still dark. She started the day by cleaning up the toys that Graham had loaned them before Dillon was awake to see and putting them all back neatly into their storage containers.

Dillon slept until nearly nine, so she managed to clean the kitchen and one of the bathrooms, packing his clothes and things as she went. She gave Dillon Gerald's old suitcase instead of his paper bags. He was going home with a lot more than he'd arrived with and the suitcase camouflaged that better than the paper bags would have. It would have been far more obvious that the paper bags had multiplied and she did not want Melinda to make a production of refusing the purchases on principle. Not that she would.

Dillon ate his Eggo waffle with satisfaction. Then he ate two more, smiling at them and poking his fingers through the holes before he consumed them. Eggos had been a good choice and she congratulated herself internally, feeling immensely proud to have fed Dillon something he would actually smile at that hadn't even been on Melinda's list.

After breakfast, Carol took Dillon outside to blow some of the bubbles she'd gotten at Target. It couldn't hurt to have Melinda drive up and find them happily engaged. It made a nice picture. All the scene was missing was some fancy orchestral music and a handsome leading man.

They blew bubbles for a long time, covering the street in the iridescent spheres. Melinda did not arrive, although Carol kept watching for her. Why did people never arrive when you wanted them to? It was like how the calls you were expecting always came when you were on the toilet, or how men you were attracted to only ran into you when you were covered in children's pee.

Just as they were about to go in, Graham came out of his house. A few days ago, Carol would have assumed he was spying again. This time, she waved. Graham waved back and then looked like he had changed his mind about where he was going as he walked across the street.

"Listen," he said. "This is a little out of the blue, but how would you like to come to a little party tonight? Dinner's included. It isn't going to be much but some of my friends are coming over and I'd like it if you'd come. Bring Dillon if he's still around. You can put a note on the door for his mom to pick him up at my house."

"I'd love to," Carol blurted. Had she really said that? "Uh, can I bring anything?"

"Just yourself. And Dillon, of course. If he's still here."

"What time?"

"Make it about six if you can, but we won't start eating until seven."

"Okay, thanks for asking me. That's really nice."

Really nice? It was fucking unbelievable that he would ask her after the way that she had treated him. She wondered if she had time to find one of his books at a store in town and read it before dinner, since she'd tossed the one he'd given her away in disgust. Probably not.

Lunch was pizza again. She didn't want to risk a meal he wouldn't eat before sending him home and pizza was good for you, she supposed. It had bread on it. Bread was at the bottom of the food pyramid, the base. Dillon pulled off all the cheese before licking the sauce from the pizza. He wouldn't eat the apples this time, though. And Melinda still did not come.

Dillon and Carol took out Graham's toys again and played with them until late afternoon. Then she found some animal wildlife shows on the TV to entertain Dillon long enough for her to pick out something to wear to Graham's. *I should have asked who was going to be there*, she thought, sifting through the hangers. And was it casual? Formal? Surely not formal.

She decided to wear black jeans and a beige velour shirt with a cowl neck. With her Mexican silver jewelry, she looked just casual enough for casual, yet just sophisticated enough to fake dressy. *What, this? Oh, I dress like this all the time. No greasy hair and yoga pants here.*

She pulled her hair back in what she hoped was a stylish way. It was almost a chignon but a little too messy. One strand kept falling down. She had to choose between plastering it all down with Aquanet or allowing it to run free. Carol opted for the Aquanet, setting the bottle back down on the counter next to the Sun-In she never would have admitted to using.

Once her appearance was taken care of, she dressed Dillon in khakis and a polo shirt.

They gathered up the toys to take back to Graham's. Dillon did not want to put the little toy train back. He held on to it quite firmly, even when she offered him the lightsaber in its place. Carol couldn't decide if it was worth upsetting him by taking the toy away. She never knew how long his upsets would last and she didn't want to bring an angry, fussy Dillon to a dinner party.

"Okay, Dillon. You can carry the train over in your hand. Good idea. You can give it back to Graham personally." She nodded. Dillon nodded. What was he nodding to? Who could tell. He might forget it at Graham's house or he would fall asleep and lose his limpet-like grip on it. Either way, it was going back to Graham. She would make sure of it.

She did not feel like this was the moral high ground but she wasn't in the mood to try to seize whatever high ground there was, if any. Dealing with Dillon could feel like a moral swamp.

Carol took the box and her keys and took Dillon by the hand before stepping out into the fresh night air. There was no moon and the stars were very bright, like spilled rhinestones across a black velvet sky. Graham's house was completely aglow. It looked like every light in the house was on. There were three cars in the driveway, none of them Graham's dark blue Volvo, and there were four more parked on the street in front of his house.

Jesus. How many people were coming?

She rang the doorbell. The door was opened by a tall, dark man with curly black hair and high cheekbones and very large eyes. He was gorgeous, like a model from a magazine, only real.

She hoped she wasn't staring too obviously.

"Hi, I'm Paul. You must be Carol. Come in."

Paul took the box from Carol and tucked it under one arm while waving to people on the sofa. Carol got the impression of a roomful of men. It was very strange. She had expected couples, but there were just the three men on the sofa. One of them had his arm around the man to his right. So a gay couple, okay. All this went quickly through Carol's mind along with the thought that perhaps one of these men might have belonged to Graham.

Not that it was any of her business, of course, but she'd thought he'd been interested in her—had practically accused him of it as if he were a pervert, in fact—and if he had not only not been interested but also gay, she was going to feel even more stupid and awful than she had been already, because it was as if she had forced her own impressions on him like a label that didn't quite fit.

Happy thoughts, Carol screamed at herself, finding herself with the desire to abandon the social gathering and the dinner and just grab Dillon and run.

Carol smiled at the men. "Hello."

Introductions were forthcoming. She was smiling blankly now, and had already missed two of them in her rush of panic. The third man was named Richard, sitting in a leather chair next to the couch. She just barely caught his name, and that he was a professor of English.

Then there was Gary, snacking at the table where the hors d'oerves were laid out. Technical writer and editor. He'd also written a book called "The Type A Buddhist," which sounded like something one of

Gerald's awful coworkers would have given him as a Christmas gift. And then there was Ralph, also snacking, who was a publicist (*what even is a publicist?* wondered Carol).

Finally, in the next cycle of introductions, she learned David's name, who was bringing in chairs from another room. He was an engineer. She still didn't know what Paul did. Maybe he just wandered around looking lovely and people just paid for the privilege of looking at him.

The minute Graham entered the room, Dillon was off like a shot to grab him around the leg. Carol winced but Graham seemed pleased by Dillon's unchecked exuberance.

"Have you all met Carol and Dillon?" he asked.

Heads bobbed.

"Good. Take a seat, Carol. I've got a teenager here that I promised to pay if she would look after Dillon. Sarah—Sarah?" A girl came out of the back, who looked about fifteen or sixteen. She was very pale, very petite. Actually, she looked quite a bit like Dillon's mother, except Sarah was dark-haired and Melinda was blonde. Dillon hid behind Graham when he saw her.

But Sarah got down on her knees—much more easily than Carol herself—and crawled behind Dillon and tickled him. His mouth dropped open in surprise and one of those little startled sounds of delight escaped him. And with the ice broken in this fashion, Dillon allowed himself to be led away by the hand, the train still clenched in his other hand.

"You know, Sarah looks a lot like Dillon's mother," Carol couldn't help remarking.

"She must have had him when she was a child herself, then," Ralph said.

Carol paused. "Yes, I suppose she must have."

God, she couldn't imagine. When she was a teenager, her life was a total mess. There were some mornings that she'd been hardly fit to take care of herself, and taking care of a tiny, vulnerable human being in addition to herself would have been entirely out of the question.

The thought that Gerald might have gotten Melinda with child while she was possibly still even going to school herself made Carol feel sick to her stomach.

"So sit down and tell us about yourself," said one of the mystery men on the couch. This one was balding and had a cherubic face. The other was angular and sulky-looking.

Carol settled into the tawny leather armchair that was the mate of the one Richard was sitting in.

"Yes, tell us *all*," Paul said, as if he expected her life to be exciting.

They all looked at her hopefully.

Oh dear, thought Carol.

"I'm afraid there isn't much to tell," she said. "At the moment, I'm on leave from my job. I'm in investor relations. I, uh, live across the street. And that's really all there is to say."

She could have mentioned that her husband had just died and she'd met his new, just-out-of-her-teens/possibly-been-impregnated-*in*-her-teens fiancée at the hospital, and that she was now, right this minute, babysitting their love child. But she left that part out. Even though she figured it was probably the most interesting thing about her, which was really, really sad.

This is your life now, Carol. Dig in.

"Well, Carol-from-the-block, how did you get landed with Dillon for the evening?"

"Oh, that's a long story, but to make it short, I'm just babysitting him for a while. His mom and I are—" are what? Oh God "—old friends," she finished lamely.

"We admire you for taking on such a task," laughed Cherub Man.

Angular Man shot her a piercing look.

What did that look mean? Had Graham been talking about her? She would die if he had told them about her little meltdown on his front porch.

"We thought about adopting," Cherub Man said casually. "But it seemed to be too much. We babysit for Robert's sister sometimes. She's a single mom and doesn't get out much. It's fun but exhausting. I prefer being able to give the kid back at the end of the night. Robert says he never appreciates the quiet of our house like he does after a visit from Emily."

Robert smiled. Slightly. So Angular Man was named Robert.

"How old is Emily?"

"Five," said Robert.

"Just started school this year," said the cherub.

"Wouldn't you be worried about the example you'd set for a child?" Richard asked pointedly.

Robert glared at Richard, but Cherub Man said sweetly, "You're absolutely right, Richard. Having two successful lawyers as parents is probably more than any child could bear. They might be so overburdened by the pressure that they'd have to settle for teaching law, as opposed to practicing it."

Richard scowled.

Robert kissed Cherub Man on the cheek. "That's why I love him."

Carol felt a hand on her shoulder and resisted the urge to jump. "Have you met everyone in here?" asked Graham. "The ladies went for a walk to see some of the houses being built in phase three, but they should all be back soon."

Ah, so there *were* ladies. Carol felt so relieved.

Cherub Man laughed at the look on her face. "You thought you'd been invited to a gay orgy, didn't you?"

Heat rushed to her face, and she felt completely exposed, but before she could say anything, Graham jumped to her rescue. "Stewart, if you don't behave, I swear I'll put you in the backyard for the night, and you'll be all alone, with no drinks, no food, and no one to mess with. So be *nice*."

"Oh no, not the doghouse." Stewart smiled at Carol. "I'm so sorry. I don't know what gets into me."

He began to chuckle. Robert turned red and excused himself to get another drink.

Carol got the joke quite a bit after everyone else and when she turned red, too, Stewart began to laugh again, and this time, Robert reluctantly joined in, patting his boyfriend on the knee.

Richard, needless to say, didn't laugh.

Graham shook his finger at Stewart, who mimed locking his lips and throwing away the key.

Gradually, the talk shifted, turning to politics. Carol's least favorite subject, because it had been one of the spots in her marriage that she'd had to carefully gloss over. Gerald fancied himself a martyr every tax season, like he was single-handedly carrying the burden of the poor on his shoulders like Atlas. As soon as he started railing on about social programs and the socialist freaks from Berkeley, Carol would quietly leave the room.

"You know," Richard intoned, "I've been creating a little list at home of people who were the top contributors to the twentieth century. You know, folks like Churchill and Truman, Eisenhower, Reagan, and—"

"You've got to be kidding, Richard. Reagan was the biggest dickhead we've ever had as a President. Ronnie Ray Gun was practically senile and you want *him* on your list? The man literally napped in office. He let his wife and an astronomer—sorry, I mean an astrologist—run the country. I *wish* it had been an astronomer. At least they're scientists." Ralph shook his head in dismay. "And who can forget his stupid little joke at the microphone. 'The bombs are on the way.' *What* a guy. Figures you'd put him on your list. You probably do a fair bit of napping in your office, too."

"See," said Richard, in what was apparently his usual monotone. "This is exciting. I see Reagan as a real breakthrough president. A man who gave us back our pride in being American. And you, you see him as a dickhead. Well, *I* see him as responsible for overthrowing communism and creating the best economy we've ever had to date."

"Regan gave us back a sense of pride we didn't deserve. He gave us pride and nothing else. While he was snoozing, his henchmen were doing all sorts of illegal and questionable things in the Middle East and South America. A trend, I might add, that continues to this day. God, Richard, you can be so fucking naïve."

"But Ralph, how do you know all that stuff is true? You don't, and no one else does, either. Reagan was a lot more put together than you or the news media give him credit for. And his achievements are so vast, even a child would be able to acknowledge them. You liberal humanists are such hypocrites. You're willing to genuflect at the altar of minor historical figures and no-talent artists as long as they're ethnically diverse, but someone of real historical significance you can't even lower yourself to recognize because you might—"

"Let's have a vote," Graham said, cutting Richard off. "How many of you sniveling infants think Reagan was totally together and really on top of his game?"

Richard's hand shot up. He looked around. No one else raised their hand.

"Uh-huh. And how many of you think Reagan had Alzheimer's way before he left the office?"

Everyone else raised their hand, including Carol.

"Survey says—bzzz. You lose the feud, Richard."

"Only because you've slanted the odds by having liberal friends," Richard said, a bit sullenly. "I suppose they don't respect Bush, either. You probably still laugh at him about that incident in Japan—even though everyone gets the flu. I suppose," he went on, at slightly higher volume, "you're probably all Clintonistas who will be voting for the most corrupt administration ever."

Carol wondered if he was this bad as a lecturer. His students must need NoDoz.

"Okay, Richard. That's enough—or you're going in the backyard. What is it with you guys tonight?" said Graham. "I'm trying to show off my beautiful house and make a good impression and you're blowing it for me. No more politics. You lot never agree. I've heard it all before, and I don't want you fighting tonight. Talk about something, *anything* else."

"You took the vote," Richard pointed out sulkily from his chair.

"Why don't you go print up some more of your delightful pop quizzes," Stewart suggested, which made several of the men laugh. Richard turned red and opened his mouth.

At this point, four ladies came in through the front door.

"Ah, the deus ex machinettes," said Graham. "Gentlemen, claim your wives and let's have another round of introductions before we go through another Cold War."

Paul walked over to a petite brunette who looked remarkably like Audrey Hepburn. "This one's mine," he said and he smiled as he reached for her hand. She pulled back from him. It was fast, but Carol noticed. Paul's face gave away nothing and he continued to smile proudly.

"Ladies," said Graham. "I'd like to introduce you to my neighbor. This is Carol. Carol, this is Jeanette. She's Paul's wife. And Claire—she's Richard's wife. Beth belongs to Gary, and Rachel to Ralph. And Sarah, the girl who's taking care of Dillon, is Gary and Rachel's oldest daughter."

Jeanette was the petite brunette. Claire was tall and blonde and a little plump. Beth had a long slender nose, huge dark eyes, and a wonderful olive complexion. Her hair curled all over in a long glorious mass of browns and reds. Rachel was of middling height and a little overweight and very kind-looking. She was the only one who had on sensible shoes. Carol felt like she would get along quite nicely with Rachel. She found the other ladies quite threatening.

After the women returned, Graham put out real food on the table in the dining area and they all ate buffet style. Graham had put out "tapas." Carol wouldn't have known what that was, but she overheard Jeanette and Claire discussing it, comparing them to the real ones that they had both apparently had in Spain. According to Jeanette, they were becoming quite passe now that all of the "it" bars had glommed on to the trend (but they were still fun and wouldn't add weight to your thighs and wasn't Graham being a good host). It was quite condescending.

Carol checked her watch in the kitchen while she was helping to gather up and clean some of the dishes after pouring herself another glass of wine and found, to her amazement, that it was nearly ten o' clock. After the ladies, no one had touched the door. Where on Earth was Melinda?

She crept upstairs to check on Dillon. He was fast asleep on a bed in the spare room upstairs. Sarah was sitting on the floor beside the bed and was watching *90210*. She glanced away for a second, waving gamely at Carol, who waved back before going back downstairs, her heart beating a little faster from worry.

She could hear raised voices in the living room as she returned. Despite politics being forbidden as a topic of discussion, Richard and Stewart were arguing loudly about gay rights while the rest of Graham's friends watched them both like it was a tennis match.

Graham was wiping off the table and putting away the last of the leftover food. "If I stop them now, they'll just look for something else to fight about," he said. "Can I send a doggy bag home with you? There's more than I can eat alone."

"That's so nice," she said. "But to be honest, I overdid my shopping when I went out with Dillon. I bought *all* this food and he's going home tonight, and he didn't even eat much of it. I don't know what I was thinking. I've got too much in my fridge as it is."

"What time are you expecting Dillon's mother?" Graham asked, putting some large platters back into a cabinet over the double ovens that, Carol thought, looked an awful lot nicer than hers.

"To be honest, way before now. But his mom actually didn't say. She's young and seems a little flaky, but I know she did say Sunday and I left a note on the door. It's a big note, so she couldn't have possibly missed it, even in the dark. I probably ought to get Dillon home and ready to go. She's bound to come soon," she went on doubtfully.

"Well, if she gets back too late, she might hold off until tomorrow. She might not want to disturb you or Dillon in the middle of the night."

That sounded sensible and could account for Melinda's absence.

But Melinda, more and more, did not really strike Carol as a sensible person. She had seen the lace in those shopping bags that Melinda had tried to hide. It was, she had thought, a little bit odd that she had had time to buy herself little bits and bobs, but not to write out a thorough list of Dillon's needs before putting him into the hands of a virtual stranger.

So much of this was very strange.

"I better go," she said aloud. "But thanks so much for inviting me. I had a really nice time here."

"Thanks for coming. I usually stand out as the lonely guy at my own parties. It was nice to have someone here for a change. My friends are usually more friendly. I don't know why they chose tonight to be awful. I just wish we'd had more time to talk to each other."

What? thought Carol.

Graham came over and placed his hands on her shoulders. Carol closed her eyes and held her breath when he leaned in—and kissed her on the cheek.

What were you expecting, Carol?

She sighed. "Goodnight, Graham."

"Wait. Let me carry Dillon home for you. I bet he's asleep."

"That would be great. He was asleep the last time I checked on him."

On the way out, they walked through what looked like yet another confrontation in Graham's living room. Richard and Robert, both very red of face, were yelling at each other while Stewart lectured David on the couch, with Ralph egging them both on. No sign of the ladies. Perhaps they had decided to revolt by leaving.

"Don't kill each other until I come back," said Graham, over his shoulder. "I want to watch."

Graham carried Dillon across the street in his arms. Carol took the note off the door on the way in and whispered to Graham to take the stairs. "The first door on the right is his room. Just put him down in his clothes. I changed him before we came over. I'm not going to worry about it."

Graham left and then came back, *sans* Dillon. He said goodnight again. There was a sort of hesitation that might have meant something and then he was gone. In a hurry, no doubt, to see the bloodshed in his living room.

When she went in to check on Dillon, Carol saw that he had fallen asleep clutching the train.

Carol slept badly. She kept thinking that she'd heard the doorbell and even went downstairs several times during the night, half-expecting to see Melinda camped out on the doorstep. But she never turned up, so Carol trudged back to bed, anxious and exhausted.

When she woke up for real, it was 8:20.

Dillon was still asleep on top of the bedclothes wearing what he had worn to the party. Carol was a little worried about his diaper but not so worried that she wanted to wake him up.

While she was downstairs, wandering around, trying to think of something to keep her mind off Melinda, she heard a soft knock on the door. *Finally*, she thought, wondering even as she went to open the door why she felt a little disappointed.

But it wasn't Melinda. It was Graham, holding a pink bakery box and the box of toys.

"Donuts?"

"Absolutely," she said with relief. Now she didn't have to worry about making breakfast before Melinda arrived. "Do you come with the donuts?"

"You bet I do," he said, laughing. "There are some of my favorites in here and I want my finder's fee. Has Dillon's mom been by yet?"

"No." Her smile faded. "No phone calls, either. You know, she really doesn't know me all that well. I would have thought she'd have called at least once, just to check in. You know? Just to see how her boy is doing."

"How *is* he doing?"

"Asleep right now."

"Well, how about I wait around with you? You can tell me how you ended up with him. I brought back the box of toys, too, just in case you needed them." He jangled the box.

"I'll only tell you about it if you promise not to use it in one of your books."

"I promise," he said, a little too quickly.

"Scout's honor?"

"Scout's honor—although I'm not sure what good that will do, since I wasn't actually a scout."

So Carol told him about the hospital, and Melinda, and the police, as they sat at her kitchen table and had donuts and coffee. She left out the dreams and her diary where she wrote about wanting to kill Gerald. And she decided not to mention Ray. She had kind of forgotten about him over the last few days, and remembering how desperate she'd been embarrassed her.

"I'm sorry now that I promised I wouldn't use this for a book." Graham sighed. "Did Melinda leave you any note? A phone number? Someone to get in touch with in case of emergency?"

"All I've got is this." Carol took the medical permission note off the fridge to show Graham.

"Was she going out of town? Running errands? Did you call her apartment?"

"No, I didn't." Carol spoke slowly. "I should have. I just didn't think of it. I'll do that now."

Carol went to the office and quickly dialed Melinda's number, winding her finger through the coils of the desk phone. She still had the number memorized, as if it had been seared into her brain.

She got the answering machine.

After two more tries, Carol hung up.

"Any luck?" asked Graham.

"Just the answering machine. I was afraid to leave a message."

"Why?"

"If anything's happened to her, I don't want *my* voice on her answering machine. The police already thought I might have killed my husband. I'm sure they'd be happy to believe that I killed my dead husband's mistress or whatever she was instead."

"That's rather paranoid."

"Do you not read books, Graham?" she said, which made him roll his eyes. "Besides, you weren't there, when they interviewed me. The officer was very—persistent."

She shuddered at the memory of Officer Muller.

"Okay, fair enough. But then what if she doesn't show up at all?"

"You think she won't?"

"Flighty and young? I mean—sure. It's a risk."

"Well, then I don't know. But I'm not calling the police. I'd rather keep Dillon forever than call the police." And she would, too, she realized. She had grown to like the boy quite a bit during her week with him. She ran her hands through her hair, which was still stiff from the Aquanet. The flattened curls probably looked like a rats' nest, but she was too distracted to care. "It's not going to come to that, I'm sure. She'll be back. I'm sure she's got a good reason for being late."

Carol closed her eyes briefly, forcing a smile. "And hey," she said, "you didn't tell me if I missed any bloodshed last night."

Graham looked confused.

"You know, your friends. The fighting ones. You told them not to kill each other." She wondered if this was in poor taste, bringing that up after wondering aloud if Melinda was dead.

"Oh, right. Richard left by the time I got back. He's a sad case. I tried to drop him as a friend a couple times, but he always calls me, desperate to hang out. You can see why, I guess. At the last party he came to, he actually quizzed people. He walked around the room giving people these little 'tests' he thought they'd enjoy and then graded them right in front of them. It was a pretty grim evening. I'm not even sure where he got those tests. He must have printed them at Kinko's."

"Oh my God," Carol said. Stewart's seemingly off-handed comment about pop quizzes suddenly made sense. "You must be kidding."

"Nope. Luckily, Stewart livened things up by coming up with some fresher test questions. I remember one of them was, 'Who was a bigger drama queen? Limbaugh or Liberace?'"

Carol nearly choked on her coffee. She could easily imagine Stewart doing that, trying to ruffle the starched-up Richard and undoubtedly succeeding. She had liked Stewart. He seemed fun, and he said the types of things everyone was thinking, only he said them aloud. Richard, on the other hand, was both pompous and pathetic. She hadn't liked him at all.

They finished breakfast. Carol ate too many donuts. It was as if her mouth couldn't stop chewing because her mind wouldn't stop turning. She kept thinking about Melinda and Dillon. She wondered what the hell she was going to do.

Could she really keep him?

A noise from the hall momentarily distracted her. Dillon was awake, and had taken off his pants upstairs, so he was now just in his shirt and diaper. Graham held out the box down at his level, so he could make a selection, which Carol thought was very kind.

Dillon forewent the sprinkled donuts, choosing two old-fashioneds, which he proceeded to nibble all the chocolate frosting off of, getting chocolate all over his hands, face, and clothes.

"Have a seat in the living room," said Carol. "I'm going to clean Dillon up. Be back in a minute."

She held both Dillon's hands on the way to the bathroom so he wouldn't touch her, the walls, or anything else. She was beginning to notice gray streaks on the walls and doors at Dillon level. It wasn't pretty and would probably have to be repainted. Now she understood why Diana's house always looked the way it did. In fact, Carol was amazed that it looked so good, considering.

Graham was setting up the wooden train set in the living room when the two of them got back. Dillon helped Graham by setting up all the trees in a row along one of the tracks.

Since no trains could actually pass now, they rolled the train on the carpet beside the track. Graham chased Dillon for a while on his hands and knees with the train. Carol watched them, yawning constantly, and realized that she was really quite exhausted.

"Let's go somewhere," Graham said, finally tiring of the chase. "Let's have some fun."

Carol groaned. "I'm too tired to have fun and I ate too much. Besides, I'm sure Melinda will show up today, probably the very minute I'm gone, and I probably ought to be here."

"Why don't we drive by her apartment?" Graham suggested. "Maybe she went home before she came here and lost track of the time."

That seemed doubtful. "Isn't that creepy?"

"Only if she sees you."

"Wow." Carol shook her head. "You haven't seen where she lives. It's an awful area. I don't really want to go there again."

"I'd like to see it. I'm curious now. Indulge me. Maybe I can use it in my next book."

"Indulge you? Hmm. I don't want to spoil you. Will I spoil you if I change my mind? Will you think you can always get your own way if you beg?"

"I wasn't begging. I was negotiating. There's a difference."

"Let me guess. It's negotiating when you want something and begging if someone else does it."

"By God, she's got it," said Graham to Dillon in an over-the-top British accent.

Dillon looked pointedly at the wall.

"Okay," Carol sighed. "Okay, I give up. Let's go."

Carol, Graham, and Dillon piled into Graham's Volvo and headed off for Lutherville. Carol left another note on her front door, saying where they had gone and that they would be back soon if she, Melinda, wanted to come back or wait around. After a moment's thought, she wrote their departure time, too. The last thing she wanted to deal with was a kidnapping charge.

Dillon fell asleep in his new car seat while Carol and Graham talked about movies. She was surprised and delighted at his taste in movies, which rather than being the B-rate horror and sci-fi pulp she was expecting, was actually quite varied.

Before she knew it, they had arrived at the Palms. It looked exactly the way she remembered it, except the children and the broken wagon were gone. Now there was a man spraying weed-killer on the dying lawn, in pinkish puffs of aerated chemicals.

"What a depressing place," commented Graham.

"I told you." Carol scanned the building, looking for—what, exactly? She didn't even know what Melinda's car looked like, or if she had even owned a car. She might have rented or borrowed. Hell, maybe she even drove a bike. Carol didn't know what apartment number Melinda lived in, either. She mentioned this worriedly to Graham.

"It would probably be on one of the mail boxes."

"But I don't want to get out and look. What if she sees me nosing around?"

"I could look," he said. "She doesn't know me."

Carol thought about that. It made sense. "Okay."

Carol parked the Volvo around the corner from the Palms and Graham walked down the street to check out the mail boxes. Carol watched him. He had such a casual, relaxed gait, like he belonged there. How did he do that? She would have been tense, hardly able to uncoil her joints enough to make the trek to the mail boxes at all. And then, with her luck, someone would have noticed her acting so guilty and immediately called the police.

Graham came back to the car, shrugging his shoulders. As he slid into the passenger's seat, he said, "There's no box with anything like that name on it. Unless she's living with someone."

Gerald, thought Carol. "Was Gerald's name on any of the boxes? Anything like that?"

"No Clarks," said Graham. "No Melindas. No nothing."

"Shit," said Carol. "God. What is going on? What am I going to do?"

"Well," Graham said. "You said you would keep him."

Carol turned to give him a look. "He's not a puppy, Graham. I can't just give him his shots and put a collar on him."

Did Dillon need shots? Melinda had said they didn't have a doctor.

"Don't worry," Graham said easily. "Things have a way of working out."

"Or not," Carol muttered. "He might end up on a milk carton."

"A pessimist," Graham observed.

"A depressed realist."

"No." Carol switched the car back to drive, since Graham made no move to get back behind the wheel. "A pessimist rejects any good thing that happens to them. A depressed realist will question it, but eventually they just accept the inevitable, good or bad."

Graham laughed. "So you're accepting it."

Carol took the freeway exit back home. The clouds were forming a big, puffy wall in the distance, standing out in gold-edged contrast to the brilliantly blue sky.

"I guess I'm accepting it," she said.

Diana sat at the dinner table, staring at the slowly congealing landscape of leftover vegetables and bits of meat that had been pushed in abstract patterns across her children's plates, arranged in such a way to suggest that dinners had actually been eaten, when in actuality, they had not.

No TV until you eat your dinner. That was the rule, a rule her children constantly flouted.

She sighed.

She knew, at some deep and mysterious level, that she had failed Carol today. Good old trusty, dependable, and ever-so-slightly-uptight Carol.

She had not been impolite or even unfriendly to little Dillon and the children hadn't actually said anything at the park that was rude. She knew that, because she had been listening for it, because she had certainly been thinking unkind things herself. And if she was thinking those things, then her filterless children almost certainly were, too. From the mouths of babes.

But no, they had been good, although they had certainly laughed at him on the way home, giggling together in the back of the suburban and mocking his "whoosh" sounds. And she had merely been relieved that they had found someone apart from each other to pick on, letting her drive home in peace without screaming at them to be quiet.

She had seen them pull away from Dillon. She had even, slightly, approved of it. Dillon was odd and therefore anyone who willingly associated with him was odd. And at a visceral, biological level, she was glad her children had recognized this and were too normal themselves to want to lower themselves to be so strange and unnatural.

A baby bird, she thought randomly. That's what he was like. A baby bird. The kind that washed up on the lawns in spring on a tide of vulnerability and tugged at your heart and caused you sleepless nights staying up, feeding, and checking, only to die anyway, in a shoe box on a wad of tissue, stiff and cold. Dillon was like that. Not dying—at least, she hoped not, she told herself. But hopeless. Maybe she should have forced her children to practice some of the kindness that she didn't have, but she had not. She had just sat there, and let what happened happen.

She could hear her husband, Randall, coming down the hall. He looked at her.

"Why are you still at the table?"

"I don't know. I'm just tired," she said, more irritably than she had meant to.

"You're tired?" He scoffed. "What about me? I'm tired. I'm at work all day. What do you have to do?"

"Look, I just said I was tired. This isn't a contest. I know you're tired. Do you want me to list everything I did today on a sheet of paper so you can check it off and tell me if I have a right to be tired or not? It doesn't matter what you think, okay? I'm. Just. *Tired.*"

"No, I don't want you to list out everything," he said. "I just don't want you biting my head off when I come in to talk to you, you know? You're always complaining."

"Yeah, I know," Diana said to the dirty plates she was cleaning up.

She rose and began to organize them into neat stacks after scraping off the remains into the disposal. Sad to waste so much food, she thought. They really couldn't afford it.

Staying at home to take care of the children all day really stretched their resources thin.

"I only asked why you were still in here," Randall was saying now, warming to his victimhood. "I wanted you to come down and watch some TV with me since the kids are done. That's what I wanted. Not to fight over what you did or didn't do all day."

"I'll be down when I get the kitchen cleared. It's one of those things I have to do—since you asked me what it is I do all day. That's one. I pick up everyone's dirty plates and then I scrape off all the wasted food, and then I put the plates into the dishwasher. I'm sure there must be something else I do around here when I'm not sitting around on my ass, but there's three for you right there."

God, she hadn't meant to say that. Why had she said that?

Richard stalked off. She thought she heard him say "bitch" as he went, but it was quiet and she wasn't about to ask him to repeat it.

Diana went back to the dishes and began to scrub viciously, thinking about dead baby birds again. But this time, all of them wore the face of her stupid husband.

Upstairs, as if sensing the hostility, she heard her children begin to fight and scream.

WEDNESDAY APRIL 17, 1992

Christopher Hodges (CR to his friends, because his middle initial was R and there was another "Chris" in his friends group) sighed as he thought of the slim hitchhiker with the golden hair.

Mrs. Hodges turned to give him a long look.

"What on Earth are you sighing for? We're going to visit *your* mother."

Indeed they were, which was why he'd tanked himself up well and good in anticipation of this event. CR tried to keep his beer-fuzzed mind on the road and not on that young woman's slim ankles and white skin. And her feet. She'd had the most beautiful feet.

Mrs. Hodges was saying something CR couldn't quite catch. She was large and had leathery ankles with creases, and her feet were horrible. Her toes, rebelling from years of being stuffed into the tight triangular corners of fashionable 80s heels with the entire weight of her body resting upon them, had brightly colored bumps (crimson, pink, brownish-red), horny yellow toenails, and an odd smell. Her feet smelled of sweat and mildew and something else. CR wasn't quite sure what the smells were, but they always made him turn his face away.

She always cringed and whimpered when she took off her shoes, which made CR wonder why she wore shoes that made her feet feel so bad. But God help him if he ever offered such an opinion. It was none of his business, having opinions—unless they were her opinions, and then he was welcome to as many as he wanted.

The hitchhiker had small, dainty toes. The tiny nails had been painted a pale shade of pink. He could remember the blue vein that snaked across the top of her foot. She had been wearing thong-style sandals through which he could see all of her feet. It had been hard to drive.

He'd fantasized about pulling over to the side of the road and overpowering her, just like in a porno. He would have liked to have tied her up and explored her feet with his tongue while she begged him to stop. This was something Mrs. Hodges never would have permitted, even when she didn't have such repellent feet. Not that he had ever asked. No. Out of the question. That wasn't the sort of question you put to someone like Mrs. Hodges. Not if you wanted to keep both of your balls.

He would have liked to have tied the hitchhiker to the car somehow. Or maybe tie her arms behind her, so her full breasts jutted out, and then he would have stripped her naked before he started licking at her ankles, working slowly down to her feet, until he got to those perfect toes. Then he would have given her the ride she was begging for. Oh, yes. He would have.

"Christopher," Mrs. Hodges bellowed. "You do not have your eyes on the road. Remember your license!"

He pretended to yawn. "I'm sorry, dear. It's all the driving I've been doing for the new store. I'm just worn out. I'll go to the DMV this weekend and get it renewed."

Mrs. Hodges yawned.

"Just try not to kill us both."

MELINDA

When Melinda left Carol's house, all she felt was release. She was free. Free, free, *free*.

She was also burning up with jealousy. Why did Carol have all those nice things, all that room, all that stuff? She certainly didn't deserve it. She was a total loser—and a patsy. Melinda hadn't expected getting her way to be that easy. She had not expected Carol to just take Dillon without asking any—well, *many*—questions. And to believe her about Gerald! She wanted to laugh.

How sweet was that?

She thought she would have to work on the old lady for a while. Get on her good side, maybe do her a few stupid favors. But then, Melinda's whole entire life had been filled with the unexpected. For nine months, that thing had literally been Dillon. She never thought she would have gotten pregnant by her first boyfriend. Sue Williams, her closest friend at the time, had told her that you couldn't get pregnant if you were a virgin, and Sue Williams slept with everyone so Melinda had stupidly believed her.

She also hadn't expected that her parents would be so angry, or that the stupid baby would be so fussy and horrible and needy. Dillon was the worst thing that had ever happened to her.

Ever since he came around, it had just been one surprise after another. Bad luck. Melinda was absolutely convinced of that. Bad luck that she didn't deserve. Carol obviously had good luck, which she also didn't deserve, which was proof that the universe was a bastard.

Well, Carol could keep Dillon for a while and see what bad luck really looked like. In fact, the bitch would be lucky if she ever came back at all. Ha!

It hadn't occurred to Melinda that Carol might think Dillon was Gerald's son. If it had, she would have found that really amusing, but it hadn't. So many things never occurred to her, which was life was always surprising her, both good and bad.

Melinda was in a hurry as she drove back to the Palms in the car she had borrowed from Mrs. Nye. She had to promise to do Nye's shopping for a month to get the damn car. Stupid old bitch. She wouldn't do it, though. It was hard enough to act like she *meant* to do it.

She went into her apartment and picked up her stuff. She had thrown most of the good clothes she had into paper bags, along with the new stuff she had bought at the mall with Gerald's money. Going to the kitchen, she grabbed a six pack of Dr. Pepper from the fridge to help keep herself awake on the long drive.

She couldn't wait to see Dwayne again.

She hummed *Like a Virgin* as she threw some dirty dishes into the sink. She knew she should wash the dishes now because otherwise they'd be awful when she got back. There was already a nasty rotten milk smell from the cereal she'd crammed into Dillon before dragging him over to Carol's. But she didn't care about the dishes or the smell. She wouldn't care if she never saw this stupid dump again.

Still humming, Melinda locked the door to the apartment and took her bags down to the car. From there, she made her way through the midmorning traffic to the freeway. She had toyed with the idea of telling her neighbor where she was going, but what was the point? Mrs. Nye might change her mind about lending Melinda the car if she knew how far she was *really* going and she didn't want Carol to contact her. She would probably freak out the first time Dillon crapped his diapers. No, the bitch could take care of things herself with all that money she had.

God, Carol was such a bitch. Talking to her like she, Melinda, was such an idiot. Carol was the idiot. She couldn't believe how Carol had swallowed everything she had been told. Wow. How could you be so dumb and have all that stuff? Amazing that nobody had robbed her blind. The moron.

Melinda shook her head.

She would have asked questions if anyone had tried to feed her a story like that.

She couldn't believe how good it felt not to have Dopey Dillon fussing in the back seat. That was what she called him, Dopey Dillon. Sometimes he even smiled at her when she said it, because he was stupid, too. She also called him "Dillon, you little fucking bastard" or "Dillon, you 'tard," sometimes punctuated with a slap when he was really annoying her, on account of that was what he was. She thought he ought to know, since she didn't believe in sugar coating the truth.

He and Carol deserved each other, as far as she was concerned. They were both stupid, gullible morons. Maybe she *should* just leave him there. "Merry Christmas, Carol! It's the stork. Goodbye!" What could Carol really do? She could turn him over to social services, but Melinda had already thought of doing that herself and probably would have if she wasn't so sure she would get into trouble over it somehow. So maybe that would be the answer. Leave Dillon with Carol and she could deal with him forever. Fucking bitch.

"Fucking bitch," she said to herself, out loud.

Melinda let her hand lie flat out the window, against the wind. It felt good to be moving. It felt even better to have her hair coiling in the corners of her mouth and tickling across her lips. It was like she was young again. Not that she was old, but people *acted* like she was old. Having a kid made people act that way, she'd noticed. You were one way without the kid, a sex kitten, a hottie, but as soon as people saw the kid or heard about the kid—boom. You were a mom and nothing else, which was gross.

It had been so strange meeting Carol in the hospital. And it had been so fun staying with Gerald. He had been stupid, too, but at least he had been nice. Carol had just been a bitch. Melinda had known she would be. Gerald had talked about her in that tired way her dad had used when talking about her mom with his friends. It was the kind of talk where everything sounded okay on the surface, but you knew he was worn out 'cause the wife was such a bitch, even if he didn't flat-out say so.

And she knew that Gerald was just like her dad and Carol was just like her mom. She could spot people like that because she was smart. Dwayne had always said that she was a good judge of people. Or maybe he hadn't said that, but she knew he was thinking it, and that was basically the same thing.

Dwayne, she thought, and sighed.

She had seen Dwayne and known right away that he was The One. She had known he was cool and that he would be the best boyfriend ever.

And pretty soon, if she had her way, he would be the best husband ever, too.

He had been sitting on a brick wall smoking and watching her as she went by the first time they'd spoken. He had watched her every day for a week but that day, as he sat there smoking, he finally said something. She had been afraid to say anything to him. She had only been a freshman. She knew *about* him, but she didn't know him. He was always in trouble. Everyone knew who he was, but not many people knew *who* he *was*. Melinda had intended to find out.

"Hey," he'd said. And then, "Yeah, you," because she had involuntarily turned to see if he was talking to someone cooler behind her. She couldn't believe he was talking to her.

She had walked over to him. Slowly. Wondering why she was so lucky to be singled out.

"So what's your name?" he'd drawled.

She had told him.

"You wanna go out on Friday night?"

She knew her parents would never agree to let her go out with such a dangerous-looking boy. Her mother hated boys, especially the exciting ones, especially if they had piercings and wore leather jackets.

And she was always giving out stupid advice. Her favorite was, "He'll never buy the cow if he gets the milk for free." Gag.

Dwayne had long, lank, dark hair and high cheekbones, just one ear piercing, and a tattoo on his hand of a black widow spider. The tattoo scared her, but it excited her, too. She agreed to go out with him and told him to pick her up on the corner so her stupid parents wouldn't see.

Some of his friends had walked up right after she had told him she would go out with him, so Melinda figured she had been dismissed. She stood for a few moments, her heart beating very fast and her mouth dry, completely ignored, as if she hadn't even been there.

Then she realized that she should just go away. She had felt pretty stupid for not realizing that a few seconds earlier. So she could have been cool and left right away, like hot boys asked her out all the time. It would have been great to say yes and then turn away immediately. She knew that's what she should have done. And then he could have seen how good her butt looked in her tight jeans. But he couldn't even see her walk away now because his friends were in the way.

She told Sue Williams that Dwayne had asked her out, but Sue hadn't believed her. "You?" she'd laughed. "But you're just a freshman." Sue could be a big bitch. But she was fat and probably jealous. That's what Melinda had figured. It wasn't easy to get boys to go out with you when you were fat and had stuff written about you in the bathrooms about how easy and desperate you were. Sue was a good friend, though, because whenever they met boys, Melinda always got first choice of who to flirt with because nobody ever picked Sue. She got what Melinda chose to leave her, and that was just the way it was.

Sue could also do a wicked imitation of Melinda's mom that was funny. Sue would purse her lips and lift one eyebrow and say one of the stupid little things her mom was always saying, like "whores use blush, ladies pinch." Whenever Sue and Melinda went to the mall to go clothes shopping and to look at makeup, Sue would cock an eyebrow and say in a nasal bray, "Ladies pinch" and "a girl all wrapped up in herself makes a pretty small package." And then they would both crack up until one of the store clerks told them to leave.

Melinda had waited out in the dark for Dwayne to show up that Friday. She had climbed out of her bedroom window. It had been easy to go to bed early. She just told her mom that she didn't feel well and that she'd had bad cramps. Then she'd lain down fully dressed in her jeans and a white t-shirt trimmed with lace under her white chenille quilt with the pink roses on it.

When she was sure she could not possibly wait another minute, she made a mound of pillows in her bed so it would look like she was sleeping and then she slipped out the window into the dark. She'd had to climb the back fence but she had been doing that since she was a kid and had plenty of practice. She had twisted her ankle a bit jumping to the ground, but in the rush of her excitement, she'd barely felt the throb of it.

And then she had stood on the corner where she'd told him she would be, standing in the dark. Waiting for Dwayne under the cold stars. She could feel every part of her body in the dark, how every breath seemed to fill her whole body. She felt like she had been waiting her whole life for exactly this kind of night. But—

He'd been late.

Every car that passed excited and terrified her. She thought she was going to explode right there on the corner.

When he finally did show up, he had two friends in the back seat.

"Get in," he'd said.

She did. Dwayne and his friends continued a long and involved conversation about motorcycles that they had been apparently been in the middle of before picking her up. They were discussing something to do with engines. Melinda didn't understand it at all, so she stayed quiet, trying to hide her disappointment that he hadn't come for her alone.

One of the guys in the back handed her a beer. Melinda hadn't realized that they were all drinking beer. Even Dwayne had one squeezed between his thighs. Every once in a while he would drink from it hastily, his eyes darting around for cops.

"You got a joint?" Dwayne called out to the back seat. "Send it up here."

A joint was handed up from the back seat.

"God, you guys are such dickheads. I get this stuff for you and you're going to keep it all to yourselves back there. Dickheads, God." Dwayne shook his head, as if amazed to discover that his friends were dickheads. There was a chorus of rowdy drunken laughter from the back seat. One of the dickheads kicked Dwayne's seat. Dwayne lashed out with an arm and hit the guy, hard.

"Goddamn motherfucker," shouted Dwayne. "Leave my fuckin' seat alone. I paid for this car."

Melinda settled back in her own seat. She had decided she was going to enjoy this new freedom from her parents. The freedom of being in a car with a guy who drank and smoked joints while driving and who called people dickheads and motherfuckers in his car, that he had paid for. It was thrilling. It was so adult.

Their destination turned out to be an old field in the middle of nowhere. There was a tire swing hanging from an old oak tree and around it were bunches of kids from school. Cool kids, kids who had never spoken to Melinda. Now, in the presence of greatness, they talked to her. They said "hi" or "hey."

Everyone knew Dwayne and she was here with Dwayne. It was the best.

After two or three more beers, she hadn't really been keeping track, she and Dwayne left. She asked about the friends they had arrived with. Shouldn't they wait?

"For those dickheads?" Dwayne scoffed. "They can get their own fuckin' ride home."

That was good enough for Melinda.

The car seemed to rocket through the night. Melinda realized she'd had too much to drink when she realized she could feel every jolt of the car hitting potholes and dips. She felt sick and the lights that spun past the car and threw ever-changing shadows across the interior only made her feel worse. She closed her eyes and hugged her stomach.

Dwayne must have taken this as a sign that she was hot for him because he pulled off the main road, down a backroad that lay between two pastures, and suggested they move to the back seat. Melinda didn't want to be a prude. She realized she had to do this. It was the price of going out with Dwayne. But she didn't want to barf on him, either, and if he was on top of her, she might.

"I think I'm going to be sick," she moaned.

"Shit, get away from the car, then," said Dwayne.

Melinda had barely heard him. She opened the door and stumbled down a slight incline into a thicket of weeds. She threw out a hand to steady herself against a nearby half-rotted fence as she threw up what was left of the beer in her stomach.

Dwayne came over with an old car towel and stuck it out to her.

"Here," he said. "You might want to wipe your mouth."

Melinda fell completely in love with him right then. Sue failed to see this as the grand romantic gesture that it was when she had told her about it later. "Stupid," she said. "He just didn't want you getting into his precious car with barf on you. I bet it was covered in motor oil."

"That isn't the way it was," Melinda snapped, who thought she knew a lot more about her date than Sue did, who hadn't even been there.

Dwayne had kissed her goodnight very gently on the cheek, which Melinda had thought was very romantic.

"Well, you wouldn't expect him to tongue you when you'd just barfed, would you?" sneered Sue. "Jeez, you can be so thick, you know."

Melinda had seriously started thinking about ditching Sue now that she had found real popularity with Dwayne. Sue was becoming a real drag because she was always down on Dwayne, and Dwayne was Melinda's new favorite subject. Sue thought he was a scuzzy loser with weird hair, which was funny, considering what an ugly dope Sue was.

Melinda had eventually dropped Sue, sort of. Of course, that was after she and Dwayne had started doing it. Which hadn't actually been that much fun. But it had been fun to recount it to Sue in great detail. Actually, in greater and more enthusing detail than the facts warranted.

It had hurt quite a bit. Melinda hadn't been sure Dwayne was doing it right, but since she was a virgin, she felt funny asking someone who had so much obvious experience if he knew what he was doing.

And then Sue had given her the clearly incorrect opinion that you couldn't get pregnant if you were a virgin. Because she had only done it the once with Dwayne without a condom. He had started bringing them after the first time. So Melinda blamed Sue for the pregnancy and not Dwayne. Of course, Sue had stated her opinion after the fact, but it was still her fault.

Melinda's dates with Dwayne were mostly driving out to a field and doing it in the back of Dwayne's car. He never took her out, which wasn't really his fault. He'd been banned from the mall and the movie theater. But she never got to go back to one of those parties at the field again, although she would have liked to. Once in a while, he let her sit with him at school on the brick wall that encircled the campus, but only when his friends weren't around.

It was Sue who had noticed that she was putting on weight. Melinda had noticed her clothes were tighter but she hadn't realized that she was the problem. Sue noticed things like that probably because she was always dieting and was totally fixated on what everyone else weighed and what size people were. Sue was the one who had bought Melinda the pregnancy test.

Even though they weren't really friends anymore (at least, in Melinda's mind, they weren't), they cut class after lunch and had gone to Sue's house. The test was positive. Melinda was not as upset as she thought she might be. After all, she had expected that Dwayne would marry her. And she thought babies were cute, just like little dolls.

Sue rolled her eyes. "You *have* to get an abortion."

Nothing had turned out like Melinda expected. Her parents were furious. Dwayne's parents were furious, after her parents had called them. Dwayne wouldn't speak to her anymore. The other kids pointed at her and called her a dumb slut and a whore. Melinda's parents pulled her out of school and hired a tutor for her at home when she refused to go back. Melinda's brothers quit talking to her. It was like she had the plague. No one called, no one came over, no one wanted to talk to her. And her dad kept going on and on about how she should get an abortion, how she was ruining her life. He arranged a trip to the Planned Parenthood clinic in Readley. Baxter, where she lived, didn't have one. Before the trip, Melinda decided to run away. It seemed noble. She was saving Dwayne's baby from her evil parents. She was so sure he would be eternally grateful. She knew he would wait for her. She knew he wanted to see her as badly as she wanted to see him.

The last straw was when Sue had come over to tell her Dwayne, who was eighteen, had been arrested for dealing at school. Apparently one of the really cool new kids had been a narc, and Dwayne had sold him a few pounds of pot, some hits of acid, and some coke for a party. But the party was over, as far as Dwayne was concerned. It looked like he would be away for a while.

Melinda made Sue promise not to tell anybody anything about where she was going—not that she knew where that would be. Melinda had hinted about Hollywood, letting Sue imagine the rest. Sue had promised, but only after Melinda threatened to kill herself if Sue told her parents. Melinda took Sue's address with her and promised to write, but she knew she wouldn't.

That night, she had stolen all the money in her dad's wallet and her mom's purse, as well as some of her mom's nicer jewelry, before sneaking out her window for the last time. She filled a pillowcase with everything she thought she'd need, and put the pillowcase in her backpack.

She headed for the interstate. She planned to head west and live on the beach in a bungalow.

She was picked up by a middle-aged man in a Cadillac. He was bald and had a face like a pig. He wore big glasses like her father but was way uglier than her father. She wanted to sit in the back but he insisted that she sit up in the front because he wanted to talk.

And talk he did, going on and on about his stupid life.

Melinda put on her polite listening face and had tried to actually listen. It was better than wasting precious cash by paying for a ride, she thought. And he'd bought her breakfast, too.

As she ate her McDonald's hashbrowns, the man lectured her several times about the dangers of hitchhiking. Melinda began to think he was some kind of serial killer who got off by lecturing his victims before raping and killing them. The danger almost made him seem interesting but unfortunately, he wasn't a serial killer, just a naggy old man. He dropped her off on the outskirts of Cookton and wished her good luck. He even gave her a twenty after urging her one last time to go home, to wherever she'd "run off from."

She took the twenty, but not his advice.

It didn't take her long to catch another ride with another trucker. He gave her a lecture too. And he was smelly and spit when he talked. So she got off in Lutherville when he got off the interstate to fill up, breathing in huge gulps of clean air like she couldn't get enough.

She had spent her first day in Lutherville looking for a cheap place to stay that wouldn't ask questions. She finally found the Palms, which would take her with only one month's ret. The guy who called himself the apartment manager ran his hand over her ass as he followed her to the room.

"You don't have the rent, don't worry. We can come to some arrangement. Know what I mean?" he said, with a smile and a wink.

He had curly brown hair, a weak beard, and a scrawny mustache. He was also fat and wore a white t-shirt over dirty Levi's that didn't cover his crack when he bent over. He was disgusting. He was worse than the pig-faced man who had given her the ride. This guy smelled of old beer and sour sweat.

Melinda smiled back sweetly. "I'll have the rent." Then she had added "asshole" under her breath, for good measure.

She signed the rental papers using a new last name and a fake birthday. It didn't seem to bother Cody, the manager, that she had no ID. She found out, as time went by, that most of the tenants here had no ID, since most of them were illegals, and that Cody made a huge amount of money under the table by taking a cut from the payment they got when he found them work.

He walked her back to her apartment and left her there with a key at number 17F. She wondered how many keys they were. He probably had one, too. But at least there was a chain and she would make sure to put the chain on every night.

The apartment was awful but at least it had been hers. It was a one-bedroom. The door opened into a living room, which was carpeted in olive green shag. There were holes in the carpet where you could see down to what looked like burlap and the place stank of cat piss. The kitchenette had a refrigerator but the door wouldn't stay shut, so there was a kitchen chair backed up against it to keep it closed. The place came "furnished" which meant the chair, a shabby wooden table, a brown velvet love seat covered in stains and cigarette burns, a gold easy chair without a seat cushion, and an octagonal Mediterranean-style end table. The bedroom only had a dirty stained mattress on the floor. The bathroom was filthy and covered with spiderwebs of mildew and mold. Everything was dirty. The mirror was dirty and broken. It looked like someone had kicked the door to the vanity in the bathroom in a fit of rage, as it was all dinged up—probably because they had to live *here*, Melinda thought wryly. But the toilet flushed and the water ran. It didn't run strong, but it ran.

Melinda decided to sleep on the love seat, as it looked a lot cleaner than the bed.

She had bites all over her the next morning. She had caught some fleas on her leg and rolled them to death between her fingers. Her brother Ted had showed her how to do that when they were kids. You could roll the legs right off them, which she did with vicious pleasure.

The first thing she needed was a Bug Fogger to kill the bugs. She didn't know if they killed fleas, but it was worth try, and there were plenty of other things in this place that needed killing. Melinda found some paper and a pen in her purse and started to make out a list. She put Bug Fogger at the top. Then cleaning supplies. Then food. And then: "find a JOB."

She went out early the next morning to explore the neighborhood of Lutherville. Not many people were up that early but there were groups of Latino men standing around on the corners. She later found out that they were waiting to be picked up for work. But the first day she had walked past them warily, clutching her purse, expecting them to attack her at any moment.

There was a 7-11 across the street and down two blocks. Everything was way more expensive in there than at the supermarket where her parents had lived, but Melinda hadn't seen a supermarket and the convenience store was close. Melinda didn't plan on eating much, anyway.

At the 7-11, she bought Bug Foggers, bathroom cleaner, some white bread, a pack of cheese slices, and a six-pack of soda. She asked the Indian guy at the counter if they were hiring, but he looked her over and said no, which pissed her off. He did tell her that he thought a restaurant a few blocks away might be looking for waitresses. Asshole.

She took her purchases back to her apartment and set off the three foggers. She had bought too many for the space, but she figured it was better to have too many than too few.

She found work at Richy's Steakhouse. It wasn't a bad place to work at, she had thought. The owner had a huge fat wife and a soft spot for pretty girls.

She knew right away that he wanted to sleep with her. When she first started working there, he was always catching her in the walk-in when she was getting salad or milk. He'd press up against her trying to reach something on the top shelf. Or he'd rub past her in the hallway, letting her feel his tiny stub of an erection. And he was always watching her.

When he realized she didn't object to any of this, he'd come into the walk-in fridge to kiss and grab her titties, which had gotten bigger during her pregnancy. Richy apparently got off on this sort of thing, because he'd jerk off while sucking on them. It was kind of exciting considering Mrs. Richy was the hostess and floor manager and there was always the risk of being caught, even though Richy was sad and kind of gross. At least he didn't smell.

She and Richy eventually worked out a mutually satisfying arrangement where she blew him a couple times in the walk-in while letting him play with her tits, and then he'd slip her an extra hundred every other pay period. And since it was all in cash and she was an under-the-table employee, she didn't have to give a real name or social security number, so none of it was taxed. So that was cool. And best of all, she could do all this stuff while pregnant.

She had dated a little, but she never found anyone as perfect as Dwayne, and most really cool guys didn't want to date a pregnant girl anyway, unless it was some kind of fetish thing.

Time went by. She had the baby—and he really sucked.

He cried all the time. She was lucky that her neighbor seemed to like him. Or liked him enough to take care of him for a little extra cash while Melinda was working, anyway. There were nights when she only got about three hours of sleep because the little fucking bastard wouldn't can it.

Mike, the dishwasher at Richy's, had been cool for a while. He had the biggest dick she'd ever seen outside of porn, but he was really tall, so maybe that was why. She dated him off and on for about a year. He didn't mind about the baby, but he'd broken things off with her when he found out about Richy and the walk-in. He'd walked in on them to see Richy's head buried in her open blouse with his dick in his hand. And then he'd quit. Or maybe Richy had fired him. Melinda wasn't sure, but she missed the free dinners he'd used to buy her.

She had only found out about Dwayne by accident, a couple years later. Life was funny like that. Sometimes the best things just came out of nowhere.

She had been waiting on a biker sitting at the counter one day when he suddenly recognized her from school. Turned out he was one of Dwayne's friends and he was on his way up north to see Dwayne. Dwayne, he told her, had finally gotten out of prison and now he was living with some friends up on Summit Crest near the Oregon border. She got him to tell her where Dwayne worked—in a motorcycle shop with the brother of a friend from prison, apparently. She told the biker to tell Dwayne "hi" for her. She worried for a while that "hi" might have been the wrong thing to say, but now it didn't matter. She would be able to see him person and straighten everything out and convince him she was the girl of his dreams, and the two of them would be able to continue exactly where they had left off.

Gerald had been the icing on the cake. He'd been sitting in Richy's one day, staring dejectedly at a barbecue sandwich. She'd walked by and asked him if everything was all right. She didn't usually do that, because she didn't really care, and hearing people complain when the answer was "no" really pissed her off. If they could afford to eat out, what the fuck was there to complain about? But he'd been OK-looking and he had a nice suit on. She hadn't even been his waitress.

He'd been chatty. He was sad about his wife, who he'd said was a cold fish and a bitch. Nobody understood him, blah blah blah. When he asked her out for a drink after work, she said yes, figuring she could maybe at least get a free dinner out of it.

He'd gone on some more about his wife and how she didn't really care about him, and how she'd let herself go just to spite him, before moaning about his boring job and how they were sending him to Taiwan. Melinda hadn't been paying much attention because a cute guy at another table was staring at her on and off, and he was much more interesting than poor sad Gerald.

But then Gerald had gotten all slobbery and thanked her for being a good listener. Melinda had invited him back to her place because she figured if he passed out she could take some money from his wallet. He looked like he might not miss a few bills. And if he didn't pass out and wanted to fuck her, well, there might be money in that, too. She'd seen the name on the credit card he'd used to pay on the way out. Men like Gerald Clark would pay a lot to hide their indiscretions from their fat nagging wives who had let themselves go, she figured.

But when Mrs. Nye had brought Dillon back, he'd gotten all weird. Like he'd realized he'd made a mistake and wanted to leave. Fucking Dillon always ruined everything. So she'd asked Gerald if he could at least go to the store for her and pick up some diapers and food. She'd stuffed a twenty in his hand and he'd run out without his jacket and wallet, he was that eager to leave, which was great, because it gave Melinda a chance to go through both.

He had two hundred and seventy-eight dollars in cash, so Melinda took fifty-eight, figuring he wouldn't notice. The woman in the picture with him must have been the wife. *She really is fat*, Melinda thought, turning away in boredom. She flipped through his credit cards, which she didn't dare touch, an auto club card, and some business cards—she did take one of these—as well as some other people's business cards, some in foreign languages.

She put the wallet back into his pocket and waited for him to come back. When she heard the sirens, she hadn't put it together with Gerald's delayed return. That shit was par for the course around here, where a loud noise could just as soon be a gunshot as a backfiring engine from someone's old crappy car. She went outside to look at what was happening with the rest of the nosy neighbors, wondering if there had been another shoot-out. You couldn't see anything at first because a firetruck was parked at an angle across the street, blocking the view from where she was. An ambulance was parked in front of the fire truck and a body was being loaded into the back. As the ambulance drove off, she advanced with the crowd and finally saw Gerald's car half-up on the sidewalk, rammed into a pole.

"I know him," she blurted excitedly. "That's Gerald. Gerald . . ."

The crowd was thrilled by this.

"His wife," people started yelling. "His wife's here."

A policeman walked over to the crowd and asked Melinda to come with him, which scared her at first, until she realized that he thought she was a grieving widow.

Other policemen were gathered around the owner of the 7-11, the same one who'd denied her a job and pointed her to Richy's.

Melinda smoothed her hair and asked the dark-haired policeman (who was very good-looking, just like Pierce Brosnan) what was going on.

"Do you think you can identify the man who was driving this car?"

"Yes," she exclaimed. "I can. His wallet's at my apartment."

"Are you his wife?" the policeman asked.

"No, but we're engaged." Now why had she said that? But no, this could be good. Maybe now she could keep all the money in the wallet. After all, she was engaged.

After assuring the policeman that she would meet up with him at the hospital, she raced back to the Palms and woke up Mrs. Nye.

She further embroidered upon her engagement story to Ann, managing to squeeze out a few tears, and she had agreed to watch Dopey Dillon in "her time of need." It was hard not to laugh. She took Gerald's suit coat with her to the hospital in a taxi, paid for with her "fiancé's" money. She removed the picture of Gerald and his wife from the wallet and took the rest of the money, too.

Gerald could blame the disappearance of his cash on Lutherville's finest, she thought. Everyone knew policemen always stole everything. Or the people who worked at the hospital. She bet they were all into stealing, too. How could they not be, surrounded by all those stiffs?

At the hospital, she ended up waiting quite a while in the lobby. While she was there, she tried to think over the situation rationally. No one knew about her and Gerald, so that was okay. No one was to say that she *wasn't* his fiancé. Except for Gerald, of course. And it would be fun to tell that bitch of a wife her story. She could even ask for money, say that Gerald had abused her. But that might not be legal. She didn't want to end up in prison now that she knew Dwayne was out.

So maybe she should just act the fiancée and let the wife offer her money as an apology for being duped. She figured the wife would be willing to shell out a couple grand just to go away. On soap operas, people were always offering money to people to make them go away. And she would be happy to get lost with some of Gerald's fabulous money. He looked like a big shot. She wondered how much Carol would offer her—that was the name that had been written on the back of the photograph. *Me and Carol, Christmas '89.* Sweet.

Finally, she was allowed to go up to Gerald's room. But she decided to call Carol on the way. So she dialed the number off Gerald's business card for "home." At first, she was going to say that she was calling for Gerald's wife—but then she thought she would call and pretend that Gerald had said that she was his sister. After all, if Gerald *had* been cheating, he would have lied about her. If he had been screwy enough to mention her. But men were always stupid about that kind of shit. They always slipped up, even Dwayne. So that was okay. She left what she hoped would be a convincingly sad fiancée message.

And then she went up to stand nobly beside Gerald to keep vigil.

He was so pathetic-looking. What if it had been her? What if she had gone to 7-11 to buy diapers for stupid Dillon and been hit? No one would have known. That was so sad. Who would have cared? Richy? He would have missed their golden moments in the walk-in, sure, but she was pretty sure he'd had that arrangement before and maybe even had others now.

It made her cry to think of herself lying in a hospital bed alone. If it had been her, Dwayne would never have known how much she loved him. How she'd never stopped loving him, after all this time. That made her cry harder. How unfair that would have been.

She could see herself lying with her hair spread out, looking like Cinderella or Sleeping Beauty. So beautiful, people would say at her funeral. So young. Would Dwayne have come to see her for the last time? Would he have somehow, magically found out? She was sure he would have. True love was like that. And what she and Dwayne had was true love.

Carol came in later in the morning. It went so much better than Melinda could have hoped. She really got into the character, to the point where it began to feel like she really had been engaged. And then when Gerald had died, that was just the best, because he was the only flaw in her story. If he hadn't died, he would have ruined everything.

Life, she finally thought, was finally turning around.

THURSDAY APRIL 25, 1992

She stopped at a truck stop to pee and buy some chips, but mostly she just drove straight on through to Summit Crest. She got there at about 6am.

She found a cheap motel called The Sleepy Hollow. Only $19.95 a night, and boy did she get what she paid for. Or, rather, what she didn't.

She figured it was an investment before Dwayne invited her over to his place. She wouldn't need to stay here long. She found the addresses of the two motorcycle shops in town in the yellowed, crumbly phone book provided in the room. They weren't open at seven, though, so she decided to get herself some breakfast and call a little later.

She went to the pancake house on the other side of the street and ordered a short stack and coffee and didn't leave a tip. Noreen, her waitress, had been flirting with the truckers at the counter and pushing up her big gross boobs. She didn't even offer Melinda a refill.

So in the space on the receipt where it said tip, Melinda wrote "get a life."

She thought that was very clever of her.

Melinda walked back to the motel and lay on the bed. She drank her last Dr. Pepper since the one Coke she'd had at the pancake house hadn't been enough. Then she called the first motorcycle shop. No one called Dwayne worked there. No one called Dwayne worked at the other shop, either. Melinda hung up and had a good long cry. Then she kicked the shopping bag containing the new clothes she had bought for herself at the mall and swore when she hurt her toe.

Then it occurred to her that a smart guy like Dwayne might not be using his real name. She wasn't using hers, so why would he use his? She was proud of herself for thinking of this: it seemed like proof that they were kindred souls.

So she called up both places again and asked if a guy with a spider tattoo on his hand worked there. The guy at the first place just told her to fuck off and quit calling before hanging up on her. But the guy at the second place asked her who wanted to know? So she knew she had the right shop.

"Tell Dwayne or whatever that it's Melinda calling."

She heard some loud laughing in the background as the phone was handed over but couldn't hear what else was being said.

"Yeah," said Dwayne, into the phone.

"Hi, Dwayne. It's Melinda," she said breathlessly, feeling her chest tighten up and her heart beginning to race at the familiar sound of his voice.

"Waddaya want?" he drawled.

"Can I see you?" she asked. "Can I buy you some lunch?"

"Where you at?" asked Dwayne.

"Sleepy Hollow Motel."

"What room?" Melinda could hear even more laughter in the background.

"Room ten," she answered.

At this point, Dwayne, unbeknownst to Melinda, was pretending to screw the counter, and he was making a particularly artful pelvic thrust. He had just about forgotten all about Melinda on the other end of the line as he entertained all the guys in the shop.

"Dwayne? Dwayne? Are you still there?"

There was a slight pause.

"You bet, honey. I'm here and I'll be there in a few minutes. You be ready, baby."

Melinda heard more laughter and wondered what was going on. But she was going to see Dwayne, so nothing else really mattered. "Okay—"

He hung up.

"Bye," she said, to the phone.

She looked at herself in the mirror, critically. She still looked pretty good. She unbuttoned the two top buttons of her dress. Then she put on some lipstick and a new pair of lace thong panties. She put all her crap together in the shopping bags in case he was so smitten he wanted to take her back home with him immediately. She wanted to be ready.

In about twenty minutes, there was a knock on her door.

When she opened the door, she couldn't believe it was him. He'd shaved off his hair. He looked, well, he didn't look nearly as good as she remembered. He was painfully thin, so gaunt that you could see the veins standing out beneath his skin. He looked almost like a bum. He had all these crappy stick-and-poke tattoos on his arms that looked like they'd been done by a ten-year-old and his head was all gray-looking because of the stubble. He was wearing a grimy t-shirt and dirty jeans, both stained with what looked like motor oil. He hadn't even bothered to change.

Because he was so happy to see me, she thought, but it lacked enthusiasm.

"Hey baby, happy to see me?"

Melinda bobbed her head obediently. Nothing could be further from the truth. She felt like screaming, "Who are you?" But she didn't. God, life sure was fucked up, though.

Dwayne came in and closed the door behind him before she could make a decision. "You look nice, baby. Let's have a look—" and he reached down and pulled her dress up to reveal her underwear. "Hot as ever, ooh. Let's take that dress off."

He immediately started pulling off his jeans and Melinda could see his gray jockey shorts bulging with his hard-on. There wasn't any way out of it. She'd set herself up for this—unless maybe the thought of Dillon would cool him off.

She started unbuttoning her dress. "Don't you want to see some pictures of your son first?" she asked sweetly.

"Later, baby. Later." He "helped" her get the dress off and ripped a button in the process.

Melinda couldn't wait to get this over with. How could she have remembered this creep so differently? This was going to be like fucking a street person. He smelled and he was ugly.

"Ever had it up the butt? We never did that, did we?" He had pushed her down on the brown flowered bedspread and was licking at her breasts.

Melinda started to say no and that she didn't want to start now, when Dwayne had an idea. He sat up abruptly and went over to his pants.

"I brought some cool stuff for you to try. Come here."

She got off the bed. Anything to delay the inevitable.

He got out some powder in a baggie and pulled out a piece of metal. He poured the powder out onto the metal and rolled up a dollar bill. "Take a good sniff."

Whatever, she thought, and did as she was told.

At first, she just felt like she'd inhaled pepper. And for a minute, she was annoyed. It made her sit her naked ass back down on the carpet. She wanted to sneeze.

"Now wait … wait …" Dwayne wagged a finger. "Don't sneeze," he instructed, and pinched her nose, hard.

"Ow," said Melinda.

"Come on," he said excitedly. "Let's get you back on the bed."

Melinda didn't care about the bed anymore, or about fucking Dwayne. Her face felt warm now, almost hot, and she was starting to feel really good. But she also felt like she could barely move, as if the insides of all her bones were now filled with lead.

Dwayne pushed her onto the bed and it was like she couldn't stop herself from falling. She felt like a tree. *Timber*, she thought wildly, laughter bouncing around inside her head. But her mouth was dry and it was like the giggles crumbled to dust before they could make it out of her mouth.

She was feeling really good now. Dwayne was on top of her, lunging into her, but she could hardly feel him anymore. She just felt good. Until she didn't. Until she felt sick. She tried to move Dwayne off her, but she didn't have the strength. All she could do was turn her head and throw up.

"Fuck," Dwayne shouted. "Fuck, fuck, fuck."

Now he was slapping her, but from what felt like very far away. Time was folding in on itself and she was floating above her leaded bones. There was no motel room, no Dwayne, no Dillon, no Richy. Just drifting and floating, like a little Melinda cloud.

She closed her eyes sleepily and silently willed Dwayne to disappear from her vision.

■□■□■□■

Dwayne sat on the bed and shook his head. He could not fucking believe this.

He was afraid to call 911. He couldn't get busted again. This would violate his parole and he'd go back into jail. Not state jail, either, but federal, where some big hulking meathead would probably make him his bitch. Fuck, fuck, fuck. He wasn't going to end up as some prison wet nurse, no fucking way.

He tried slapping the girl again—he couldn't remember her name. But her breathing was so shallow that he could barely tell she was breathing. And then, to his horror, it stopped.

That fucking bitch. She'd never been anything but trouble.

He wanted to call his friend John at the shop. John always knew what to do. He was that kind of guy, a fixer. But Dwayne was afraid to use the phone. He couldn't remember if they could trace local calls made from phones. He had to take care of this himself. Shit.

He found her bags of stuff. What if he stripped her and left her here with no ID? Who would know she was here? Had she told anyone? Even if she had, it would take a while for them to figure out she was missing without her things. He'd strip her, burn her stuff, and then take off for a while until the heat went down.

He wondered where she'd come from. He thought for a moment about his kid—if it was even his—but he couldn't find any pictures in her bag. She didn't seem to have any ID, either. He took her car keys. He'd have John or one of his buddies move it and chop it.

He stripped Melinda and took everything he could find. He searched the floor on his hands and knees and found that button that had popped off her dress. He took that, too.

And then he remembered DNA.

Fuck.

Fuck, fuck, fuck.

But he hadn't come and it wasn't a rape. Obviously. Maybe they'd just put it down to an OD? No, they couldn't do that, not when the body was stripped. And his DNA wasn't on file. At least, he didn't think so. Although his fingerprints were.

Dwayne went into the bathroom and wiped down everything he'd touched. Then he took off with the shopping bags after carefully checking the parking lot to make sure no one was wandering around. Then he arranged with John to have Melinda's car removed. He wasn't sure he could trust the guys at the car shop. They were the weak links. He didn't think they'd hold up very well if they were questioned. But with any luck, they wouldn't be—or if they were, he'd be long gone when the time came.

After burning up Melinda's bags and purse with a blow torch, Dwayne took off for parts unknown. He took the cash, of course. No sense in burning that.

He thought he might change his name to Spyder with a Y.

OFFICER BLACK

Officer Black looked around the room carefully. Aside from the naked dead girl on the bed, everything looked perfectly in order. The girl had checked in as Liz Smith. The manager was pretty sure she'd had a purse with her and he was very sure that she'd been dressed, although he couldn't remember in what. She'd paid in cash for two nights. No car that he'd seen.

He looked in the bathroom without touching anything. Nothing seemed to have been touched. The towels hadn't been used. The bath mat was still hung over the rail on the shower door. The toilet paper was ripped, but in a place like this, that could mean anything.

Black could hear voices outside. The town's only detective, Ron Starr, came in with a camera and an evidence kit. He had a name like a porn star and a dick-swinging attitude to match, but he was thorough. As Officer Black watched, Ron proceeded to photograph everything and take samples.

"You been walking around in here much?"

"Nope."

He knew what Starr thought of him. Starr obviously thought that he had "country bumpkin" stamped on his face. Probably thought he drove a fucking tractor with a light bar.

"Coroner here yet?"

"Don't know, but he'll have to wait until I'm done," Starr said pompously.

Well, that's obvious, thought Black.

Black went outside and stood looking out at the empty parking lot. There were no cars unaccounted for, so if she'd had a car, it was gone now. The coroner's van pulled up as Black was looking gloomily at the pancake house across the street, wondering if he dared go ask Noreen if she'd seen anything. And maybe pick up a bite, too, while he was there.

"Hey, Jim," said the coroner of Del Onofre County in his cheery voice. Bill, Sonny's tall, lanky, dark-haired assistant, waved from the front seat, but didn't get out of the car.

Black always wondered if coroner was even the right job for a man who was always so damn cheerful. His clientele weren't appreciative of his sunny demeanor, and some rigid law enforcement types found his cheerfulness downright unprofessional. Stiff upper lip and all—that was the type of joke Sonny would make.

Jim liked it, though. There were enough morose people running around out here. He ought to know. He was one of them.

"Hey yourself, Sonny. She's in there." He pointed at the door of number 10. "But you can't have her until Starr is done."

Sonny made a little face. He didn't like Starr anymore than Black did. Black figured Starr probably didn't have a single friend in the entire town, outside of his own bedroom mirror. With any luck, Starr would move out to another city like all the other big shots. He was always whining about the lack of Real Cases. And then when he did get one, he'd whine about that too. There was no pleasing a man like that.

"I'm sure he'll come out to tell you when he's ready for you," Black said aloud.

"Oh, I think we can be sure of that." Sonny smiled. "Not much more certain than that, except for shit and sunshine."

"I'm going over to talk to Noreen and see if she saw anything. Let Starr know, if you would." He tried to smile but the thought of Noreen made him grimace like he'd bitten into a lemon.

"Bye Jim." Sonny mock-saluted. "Now you tell Noreen I said hi, you hear?"

Black walked slowly and deliberately over the gravel lot that separated the hotel from the street. He was in no big hurry. He jaywalked across the frontage road towards the pancake house, which was called, uncreatively, The Pancake House. The smell of bacon and coffee hit him as soon as he opened the door. The counter was all lined up with truckers, some in vests, some in flannel, some in t-shirts. All of them were big men, with cups of tarry coffee steaming in front of them.

Dolly Parton was blasting cheerfully from the radio on the counter and one of the truckers said, "Hey Noreen, how 'bout a little sugar, honey, before I hit out on my own nine to five?"

"That'll be the day," snapped Noreen, whose rigid back was facing the door as she put up an order on the silver order wheel and spun it around for Junior, the cook. "Order up," she said, in her loud, waspy voice that always made it sound like she was on the rag. Maybe she was.

"Great," Black murmured. Noreen was bad enough when she was in a "good" mood.

"Bitch," Junior said, loud enough for everyone at the counter to hear. He yanked the order down from the wheel. Junior didn't take any shit from Noreen and she couldn't afford to let him have it since he was her boss, and there were plenty of other young things out there to wait tables.

"Why, I'm jus' talkin' about my coffee, honey. What did you think I was talkin' about?" said the big trucker. His name was actually Harry and he was on a run-up to Seattle with a shipment of Mexican flagstone tiles and Mexican statuary for a boutique Seattle retailer. Officer Black might have been very interested to know that he was also carrying a shipment of Mexican black tar heroin, cemented inside the base of a particularly handsome fountain decorated with fat cherubs and grapes. But no one, except for one corrupt operator at the boutique, and the sender, knew about that.

The counter of truckers erupted into laughter when Noreen turned red.

"You're getting blind, as well as ugly, then, Harry. The sugar's right in front of you."

The fickle truckers whistled in appreciation—except for Harry. Harry, rather red in the face himself now, got up to leave. But not before plunking down a tip. Nobody who wanted to come back and get served before they turned whiskered and grey, left the Pancake House without tipping.

Dolly Parton gave way to Billy Ray Cyrus and his Achy Breaky Heart. Jim slid into Harry's vacated seat.

Noreen's back was facing him as she pulled an order of French toast off the counter window. "Ooh, this French toast looks good enough to eat this morning, Tony. Look at that. Junior didn't burn it today. Guess you had better pay your compliments to the chef."

Junior, sweating over the grill in a stained wifebeater, glared at Noreen while mouthing what looked an awful lot like "fuck you," while Tony, at the opposite end of the counter, poured about a half-gallon of maple syrup onto his toast.

All the food was making Jim a little nauseous. He couldn't forget the dead girl's face, framed in golden hair, with the vomit trickling from the corners of her mouth in a dried-on crust. He was a bit too sensitive to be a policeman, he suspected. He never could get the images he saw out of his goddamn head, especially women and children. They came back to him at the oddest moments, and the longer he was on the force, the more images he had in his roster. He wondered if all policemen every felt this way and never talked about it. Or if it was just him and he was a pussy.

He figured that it was probably just the latter, so he kept his mouth shut.

Noreen started towards the tables on the other side of the diner and then finally noticed Black. Her face hardened and the little furrow between her penciled-on eyebrows deepened.

"What are *you* doing here?"

"Just got a couple questions, Noreen. Police business. I wouldn't have come except for that."

Noreen pursed her bright red lips, smacked them. She started to say something but thought better of it. Or else she was just saving it for a verbal hiding that would come later. She smoothed out the white apron she wore over her green polyester uniform. She'd shortened hers. It was no longer the regulation 1" above her knee. More like 8". "Better tips," she'd told him once, when they were still speaking.

The truckers, watching them, had all gotten real quiet.

Black eyed them warily. "Is there anywhere we can go that's private?"

"Junior," Noreen yelled over at the grill window. "Can we use your office for a minute?"

Junior nodded, mostly at Jim. It was the commiserating nod of a long-suffering man.

Jim gave him a wave of thanks before turning to follow Noreen into the small office where Junior kept all of the spare supplies and the paperwork. He asked Noreen, who had folded her arms in defiance, whether she had seen the petite blonde woman they'd found in the motel across the street.

"Seen her? I waited on her. The bitch didn't tip me."

"Have a little respect for the dead, Noreen."

"Did she respect me? Did she? No, she did not. She wrote 'get a life' on the goddamn receipt. I don't have to respect her." Noreen shook her heavily teased hair, patting the blonde curls with her right hand as if to make sure it was all still there. Black thought absently of the smell of her hair-coloring products. That was not one of the things he missed.

"All right, Noreen. All right. Do you remember what she was wearing?"

"Some kind of long… dress. Faded flowers, buttoned up the front."

Black made a note of that. "Do you remember her purse, her shoes—anything else that she might have had with her?"

Noreen let out an exasperated hiss and rolled her eyes to the ceiling.

Jim thought it best to move on quickly. "Okay, do you remember the last time you saw her?"

"Oh, c'mon," she said. "I got the counter and all the booths in the morning. I don't really remember. But it was before my break, so it was before 9am, because that good-for-nothing Sally wasn't here yet. And she ordered the short stack and the coffee," she added, like there was something really wrong with people who ordered the short stack and the coffee.

"No one with her?"

"Nope." Noreen popped some chewing gum into her mouth.

"She talk to anyone?"

"Nope, but she sure got some of the truckers real excited."

Snap, snap, snap, went the gum in the corner of Noreen's mouth. Jim tried not to watch.

"She use the payphone?"

"Jim, how the hell would I know if she used the payphone? It's outside. I don't got X-ray vision. She could have gone and blown someone in the restroom for all I know. I'm busy in the morning."

Snap, snap, snap.

Black winced.

"Okay, so let me see if I have this straight. She came in here sometime before nine. Did she leave before nine, too?"

"Yes," said Noreen. "Because when Sally came in, she and I bitched about the little twit."

"Okay, so she had a half stack and coffee and left before nine and you didn't see her talk to anyone or make any phone calls. Is that accurate?"

Noreen nodded.

"Thanks." He tucked his notebook away with a sigh of relief. "You've been a real help."

"So what'd she die of?" she asked, curiosity getting the better of her. "She murdered?"

"Now, you know I can't tell you anything," he said apologetically.

"Like I expected you to tell me jack."

Black was already backing away. "Well, thanks an awful lot for your help, Noreen. We might, uh, need to talk to you again." He paused and took in her angry face. "But maybe not."

He left her there chewing her gum viciously and then went table to table, trucker to trucker, asking if any of the folks in the Pancake House had seen anything at the Sleepy Hollow. Then he went over and knocked on every door in the motel asking the same question. No one had seen anything, although one couple in room 16 had a helpful suggestion about how he could sexually pleasure himself with the help of a little gymnastics.

Black walked back morosely to room 10. It looked like Sonny and Bill were working on the body. Starr was nowhere to be seen. Jim didn't see his powder blue pickup anywhere in the lot, so he figured the hot-shot had packed up his bags and gone on home to play alone.

"Hey guys." Jim stuck his head in the door. "Can I come in for a sec?"

"Sorry, Jim. No can do. This here is mine now. You'll get my report as soon as it's ready, though."

"Okay, Sonny."

The coroner, who was aligned with the county itself more than he was with the city police, locked down the scene as soon as he began his investigation. Sonny took his work very, very seriously, even if he was a cheerful guy.

Black hated these kinds of cases. They didn't have many suspicious deaths up in Summit Crest. They were a little too far north to be a part of the meth highway, with all of its little sideroads of coke- and heroine-dealing that veined through the central valley like a chronic infection. Mostly, they had car accidents. Horrible, those, and they required that the roads be closed, but they were easy to solve. People went too fast in the wrong weather conditions or they drove drunk. Sometimes a kid got lost. That was about the thick of it.

The last real murder in Summit Crest had been about four years ago when George Lapan had shot his wife for fooling around with a county clerk named Nelson D'Orazio. And that had been easy enough to solve since George had come down to the police station and turned himself in, plunking down the murder weapon and saying, "I killed the cheatin' bitch. Now lock me up."

But this case had everything that Black hated. It had a victim he really felt for: young, attractive, everything in the world going for her. There appeared to be no clues and if it took a while to solve, he'd be stuck doing legwork for Starr for weeks. Plus, Noreen was involved and wasn't that a bad omen? Black was pretty sure it was.

He got into his patrol car and cruised back to the station with the radio tuned to soft rock.

He thought about Noreen. Or mostly, he tried not to think about her. But the smoky, greasy smell that clung to his clothing from the Pancake House reminded him of her so intensely that he could almost feel her in his arms.

Of course there were all those times when she'd been in other people's arms while he'd been home alone, watching TV. Knowing where she was. And her knowing that he knew. She'd never tried to hide what she did and the fact that he never mentioned it or did anything about it seemed to be an open challenge for her. It had seemed to push her further and further, to hurt him as completely as possible.

And what no one could figure out, especially Black, was why she was the angry one. Everyone in town figured that someday Jim would kill Noreen, just like George Lapan had killed his wife. But it didn't happen—and gradually, people quit expecting it. But Jim could tell they were disappointed. Not a lot happened here in Summit Crest, after all.

Finally, Noreen up and left, shacking up with a long haul trucker named Red Clemmens. Jim wasn't sure why she left. She didn't tell him what had been the final straw. He'd been at work one day and had come home to find all her stuff gone. No note and she'd never said nothing.

So that was that.

It hadn't worked out with the trucker. But even after they'd broken up, she hadn't come back. She never spoke to him at all if she could help it. He still wondered what made her angry.

Now she lived in a trailer in the Happy Trails mobile park. She hadn't gotten remarried or had a steady boyfriend, but according to town gossip, she had her pick of the truckers at the Pancake House.

Jim, on the other hand, hadn't slept with anyone since Noreen. He hadn't meant to turn into a monk and he kept telling himself he'd go out and meet other women. He fantasized about some of the women he did meet, and he was still interested, but after Noreen, he was scared.

Don't think about it, he told himself, pulling up to the station.

Starr was off in his precious corner office, typing up his report. When he saw Black come in, he motioned him over. "Don't suppose we'll get anything but make sure you send fingerprints to state and federal and send out a description of the body, as well. Maybe someone's got a missing person case we can solve with this. Make sure you send the details to the FBI, too."

He drew in a breath. "Todd called from the local rag. I gave him the 'white female, between 15 and 25, found in motel' spiel along with a general description. Don't suppose he'll hound us, but if he makes a pest of himself, tell him to fuck off—but nicely. I asked the public to call us if they had any information." Starr bowed his head and went back to work.

Black had been dismissed.

Jim had spent a week sending out bulletins on the body and fielding phone calls from people who thought they might have seen the attractive young blonde woman, or who would have liked to have seen the attractive young blonde woman (dead or alive—he shuddered), or else from people who were just lonely and who hadn't seen anybody but still wanted to talk. There was a psychic who had called and claimed the dead girl was Bette Midler's love child, and he'd hung up on her the way he had all the other crazies.

Finally, the coroner's report came in. Death was caused by heroin overdose.

Coroner's Report:

File 60-1029

Office of the Medical Examiner—Coroner

April 1103 hours

I performed an autopsy on the body of Jane Doe at the Office of the Coroner in Del Onofre County and from the anatomic findings and pertinent history, I ascribe the death to:

ACUTE HEROINE—MORPHINE INTOXICATION

Due to: Inhalation of overdose.

Anatomical summary:

I. Pulmonary edema and congestion

II. Visceral congestion

No needle marks or evidence of morphine habit

External examination:

The unembalmed body is that of a Caucasian female, appearing about age twenty. There are no tattoos or birthmarks.

An old surgical scar is present in the right lower quadrant of the abdomen.

There is a slight amount of bloody material and vomit present in the mouth and on further examination, some disruption of the mucosa is noted. No evidence of major trauma or violence is present.

The hair is long and shows varying shades of blonde. The eyes are blue and show moderate dilation.

The external genitalia is female. There is some irregular dependent livor with the pressure changes chiefly on the right side, suggesting the body rested on the right side at the time of death.

■□■□■□■

Black let Starr do his bit but there wasn't anything here to solve the case for them.

He sighed. Why had she decided to try heroin *here*? She obviously wasn't a junkie. Why did she come here to become one? He sighed again. It was such a waste.

The internal examination revealed that she'd had a child and that she'd had intercourse prior to her death, but her partner hadn't done them the favor of ejaculating. No signs of a struggle, either. They had some DNA from her partner and maybe they could run that, maybe get lucky that way. The stomach contents also revealed that the Pancake House was the last place she had eaten, corroborating Noreen's testimony.

Not much of a last meal, Jim thought sadly.

Maybe she'd been a prostitute.

He sent out a description of their Jane Doe to every State and Federal agency on his list, but he received no inquiries about her. A local woman, Mrs. Addison, did call to ask if she could pay to bury the girl and give her a decent Christian burial. The local mortician, Alan Slade, had volunteered to donate his services, and with Mrs. Addison burying the casket and paying for the necessities, at least the girl could have a nice funeral.

The body was released to the funeral home and the funeral was well-attended. She was a pretty thing, just like a sleeping princess, and going made him sad. He was pleased by the turnout and no one even slightly suspicious attended. It was open casket and more pictures were taken, to be distributed to the media and around town in hopes of identifying her. Somebody suggested writing to *Unsolved Mysteries*, but no one took that idea seriously.

Everyone agreed that it was a lovely funeral and that the deceased had been a very pretty girl. Not everyone agreed on what she had been doing at the Sleepy Hollow. In fact, nobody agreed on that. Everyone had their own pet theory and not one of them came even remotely close to the truth.

CAROL

Carol never heard back from Melinda. Days became weeks, which became years. She began to suspect that either something terrible really had happened, or that she had been used as a means of ditching the boy. For the first couple weeks, Carol had combed the newspapers obsessively, checking the obituaries and the local news for reports about a dead or missing girl with long blonde hair, but every night, the local news disappointed her.

She considered reporting the incident to the police, but quickly decided against it. They would take Dillon away and then he would become a ward of the state, residing in foster care until relatives of his mother were or weren't found. Dillon was so different, so sensitive, and had already been through so much. Carol found herself physically recoiling at the thought of him being placed in the indifferent hands of strangers. She kept thinking of the way he had cowered from her in the kitchen, and the bruises on his legs. She couldn't bear for him to go through that again.

Instead, Carol applied for a delayed registration of birth for Dillon. She provided a copy of her marriage certificate and several other forms. She told the person at the desk that her husband had lost the papers and after he died (here, she had allowed herself to cry), there was no one left to ask. She listed Dillon's birthday as April 24th, the day he had been given to her, and applied for his Social Security card. It was an expensive process and took months. Carol found herself quite up to the task. It gave her a goal, a sense of purpose.

Her leave of absence at work became a sabbatical, and then, eventually, she gave her two weeks. There was no time to return to work while raising a three-and-a-half-year-old boy. She supposed she could have hired a nanny but the thought of turning over her house and her child (yes, her child, now) made her uncomfortable, and besides, she could afford to stay home.

She and Dillon quickly settled into a routine. She would get him ready, fix him breakfast, and let him watch TV. He liked *Sesame Street*, *Eureka's Castle*, *Lamb Chop*—anything that was a cartoon or that had puppets, he enjoyed. They went to the park or out to eat and sometimes they would visit Graham. Sometimes Graham would join them at the park or out to eat. He'd bring a leather notebook with him that he used, ostensibly, to take notes for his books, but usually it stayed shut.

In the evenings, she and Graham would stay up late into the night, talking about everything under the sun. Their favorite films, their favorite music, their hopes, their dreams. She began to wonder how she had misjudged this man so badly. What she had taken for arrogance and pride was actually just intelligence and awkwardness. Before long, they were finishing each other's sentences and making long-term plans. Soon, she found herself thinking about him the way she thought about food or air or Dillon: as something truly integral to her life that she couldn't possibly fathom existing without.

They married in the year 1996, in a quiet civil ceremony at the Clerk-Recorder's office. Graham legally adopted Dillon, who now officially belonged to Carol. And now, she thought, with delight, they all officially belonged to each other.

THE END

Ack!(knowledgements)

This was a very special book for me to write because for twenty years, it sat on an old computer, untouched. My mom wrote the first draft of this book when I was still a child myself, and when she sent it to me, it was basically still just an outline. I fleshed it out and wrote three revised drafts of it, adding an all-new epilogue and several new scenes.

She always dreamed of publishing this book, which was originally titled *An Ordinary Life*, but was too shy to put her name to it. So she gave it to me to work on and change and share out to the public. It's quite a bit different from what I usually write, but in some ways her style is also really similar to mine, and working on this book really made me feel a lot closer to my mom.

Thank you, Mom, for trusting me enough to work on your project with you.

I would also like to give big thanks to Heather Crews, who designed the book cover for us. My mom was so excited when she saw the cover that she literally shrieked. And to be honest, I did, too. I think it fits the mysterious retro vibe of the book.

And of course, a big thank you to all my readers. I am so grateful to have such supportive, passionate people in my life, reading my work. Thank you from the bottom of my heart.

And thanks from my mother, too.

About the Author

Nenia is one of those "millennials" you hear about in the news. When she's not penning smutty bodice-rippers, she's reading smutty bodice-rippers, drinking copious amounts of tea and wine, or else roaming the streets of San Francisco.

You can find her on Twitter, @NeniaCampbell; on Instagram, @alwaysbeebooked; and on Goodreads. She loves to talk to readers.